Readers love
ANDREW GREY

Fire and Fog

"Andrew Grey really knows how to give his target audience what they want. Everything about this book works for me."

—Love Bytes

"It's getting harder to pick a favorite from the Carlisle Cops series. With this sixth installment, Andrew Grey combines suspense, investigative skills, and a good mix of characters."

—The Novel Approach

Growing His Dream

"Once again Mr. Grey does an amazing job of bringing the reader into the lives of the people he is writing about."

—Paranormal Romance Guild

"Andrew Grey works his magic to bring a smile to my face and a warm and fuzzy feeling to my heart."

—Hearts on Fire Reviews

Setting the Hook

"Andrew Grey's books are a must-read in the m/m romance genre. He simply knows how to write, and gives the reader stories about everyday people living everyday lives."

—Two Chicks Obsessed

"This is a romance that is sweet, with a little bit of angst and family interference, but it is one you will enjoy tremendously. I can't recommend it highly enough. Enjoy!"

—Happy Ever After, *USA Today*

Published by DREAMSPINNER PRESS
www.dreamspinnerpress.com

Published by Dreamspinner Press
www.dreamspinnerpress.com

TAMING THE BEAST

ANDREW GREY

Published by
DREAMSPINNER PRESS

5032 Capital Circle SW, Suite 2, PMB# 279, Tallahassee, FL 32305-7886 USA
www.dreamspinnerpress.com

Taming the Beast
© 2017 Andrew Grey.

Cover Art
© 2017 Paul Richmond.
http://www.paulrichmondstudio.com
Cover content is for illustrative purposes only and any person depicted on the cover is a model.

ISBN: 978-1-64080-005-2
Digital ISBN: 978-1-64080-006-9
Library of Congress Control Number: 2017952408
Published October 2017
v. 1.0

Printed in the United States of America

This paper meets the requirements of
ANSI/NISO Z39.48-1992 (Permanence of Paper).

To Terri Brisbin, for inspiring the story in the first place. Yes… this is all your fault, and I hope you love it.

CHAPTER 1

"DANTE, YOU have to go to this dinner," Simon Yates, the attorney for the Bartholomew Family Foundation, said as he crossed the large room lined with filled bookcases. It had been Dante's father's office and was now Dante's through an unholy bargain that hung around his neck like an anchor chain.

"I arranged for the Foundation to send a check. That should be enough," Dante growled, banging his hand on the desk as he pulled himself to his full six and a half feet.

Yates paused at his outburst but showed no sign of bowing to the intimidation that Dante had been going for. Yates cleared his throat. "The check isn't going to be enough. You have a public relations problem and you know it. The little league initially returned the check from the Foundation, and the elementary schools had to be convinced to accept theirs. That isn't good. These organizations always need money, but they had second thoughts about accepting it from you." Yates shifted his weight from foot to foot. That was good. It meant Dante's tactic was working.

"If the money isn't good enough for them, then they can go without it and be damned. I'm not going to ask someone to accept my foundation's donations. Do you hear me?" he shouted, glaring at Yates. "I'm through with this. I work hard and keep most of the families in St. Giles employed and fed in one way or another. I spend a lot of time traveling to open new markets and meet with customers who will buy our products, the ones that are the lifeblood of this...." He swallowed and tried to head off the rage that threatened to boil up from inside. *How dare they!* "I keep this town running when others have fallen on hard times. And do I keep the money I make? No! I put the profits into the Bartholomew Foundation and make sure they get

1

distributed to the groups that make everyone's life better. And I ask for nothing in return other than for them to leave me alone." Dante sank back in his chair, and Yates took a step closer to the desk.

"You know the rumors that have swirled around you for years, and now they're growing and turning into a kind of town legend. People need to see you, meet you, because when you aren't growling and acting like a general asshole, you can be a personable and caring man." Yates stood his ground even as Dante lifted his gaze, seconds from lashing out. Yates was the only man who dared speak to him that way. Maybe it was because he was nearing seventy and had been his father's lawyer before the old bastard died. Or maybe it was simply because Yates had been around when Dante had taken his first steps. "Just think about it."

"Fine." Dante sighed, wishing to hell Yates would just leave. "Is there anything else?"

"I have these other potential donations for the remainder of the year that the Foundation board has reviewed for your final approval." Yates handed him the list, and Dante looked it over. "This includes the donation for tonight. There is also a venture that the board thought would be advantageous for us to undertake. The diner in town has been empty for a year, so we thought we'd purchase the building, renovate it, and see if we can find a tenant to lease it from us."

"Fine…." Dante handed the list back. "Now can I go back to work so I can make more money?" He raised his eyebrows.

"The dinner tonight is at seven. I'll be there, and we need you to come." Yates didn't budge even though Dante had clearly dismissed him.

"You're like a dog with a bone." Dante picked up a set of contracts from his desk, intending to get to work. Maybe if he ignored Yates, he'd just go away.

"Yes. And you need to do this. The people in this town haven't seen you, other than glimpses in the pottery works, in two years. You either stay in this house or come and go in that limousine of yours that looks like a glorified armored car." Yates came even closer, until he was leaning over the desk. "They call you the Beast of St. Giles."

Dante coughed and sat back, blinking.

"Ah, so you haven't heard. Well, it's true, and it's going to affect business and the people working for you. So, you have to put an end to this. Go to the dinner, smile, be charming, talk to a few people…. It isn't going to kill you."

Dante wasn't so sure of that. Allison had always been the one who went to parties and said the perfect thing while handing out the big ceremonial checks. At least she had been, at first. Dante pulled his mind away from that line of thought. He'd banned anyone in his household from speaking about her, and he needed to stop thinking about her. If that was even possible with his guilt surrounding her memory, the burden he had to carry forever.

"Probably. But what are the attendees at the dinner going to think about eating with the Beast? Maybe I'll give them indigestion." He returned his attention to his contracts. "I said I'd think about it."

Yates turned to the door. "I'll find Roberts and tell him to make sure your tuxedo is ready for tonight." He pulled open the door to leave and closed it with a thud that reverberated through the room.

Dante slammed down the contracts on his desk. He had no intention of going anywhere, least of all making some ridiculous public appearance to try to shore up his reputation. He knew well enough what the people in town thought of him, in his house perched high on the crest of the hill above the town. He certainly didn't need to hear it from them firsthand.

He sighed and went back to work—after all, there was plenty of it.

The door opened and Roberts walked in, carrying a lunch tray. He placed it on the side of the desk and turned to leave, but stopped before he got to the door. "I have your clothes for tonight prepared for you, and I took the liberty of having your car made ready."

"I'll take the limousine," Dante said, picking up a piece of bruschetta from the plate. He loved them, and Harriet made the best ones, with just the right amount of onion and the freshest tomatoes.

"It's developed a knocking, so I had it taken in for service." Roberts met his gaze when Dante looked up, hoping his feelings on that were shown in his eyes. "I have the convertible ready for you." He left the office and closed the door before Dante could say anything more.

It was a conspiracy—that was the only word for it—and he was pissed. Dante swiped his arm over the top of the desk, sending the papers flying and fluttering to the floor. He stood, stomped to the door, and threw it open with a bang that reverberated through the wood-paneled hall. He saw no one, which was probably good. Didn't anyone understand that he only wanted to be left alone? Apparently they all knew better than he did about what was good for him and what he needed. He climbed the stairs, stomping to alert those nearby that he was on his way.

Dante went to his bedroom, closed the door, and entered his private bathroom. He turned on the cold water to splash some on his face. Dante caught his reflection in the mirror and didn't like what he saw behind his eyes. They seemed cold even to him. But things were what they were and he couldn't change them. For a second he lingered, looking at himself, before drying his face and walking away.

He returned to his office to find the papers back where they'd been and his lunch laid out on the desk—Roberts being his usual efficient self. Dante sat down and ate, not really tasting what he knew was an amazing lunch. Harriet always made sure he was well fed. She was a dear, but he rarely saw her, just like he rarely saw anyone anymore.

He went back to reviewing and signing contracts, then left them for Roberts to send to the business office to be executed. His day done, he returned to his room to find his tuxedo laid out for him, along with a deep red bow tie and cummerbund. Dante groaned and looked away from the things, but sighed before picking up the tie and running the soft silk through his fingers. "All right, you old goats. I'll go." He put the tie back where it had been and went to his bathroom to shave off his five o'clock shadow—he didn't want to look like Homer Simpson—and then stepped under the hottest water he could stand for a shower.

Over the years, he'd tried more than once to wash away the stain of what he'd done, but there was no way to do that. It would stay with him forever, and he wasn't going to be able to leave it behind no matter how much he might have wanted to.

Clean, he tossed his dirty clothes in the hamper and went to his room to get dressed. He got his pants and shirt on before Roberts seemed to know he was needed and knocked softly on the door before entering.

"Let me help you." Roberts attached the gold-and-onyx shirt studs and the cuff links before tying his tie and making sure it was perfect, then helping Dante into his jacket. "You look stunning." He stepped out of the way so Dante could look at himself in the mirror.

Dante nodded, pleased with his appearance. He sat on the bed to pull on his socks and the mirror-shined shoes Roberts had set out for him.

"There. Now no one will be able to keep their eyes off you."

Dante humphed. There wasn't anyone at this dinner who was going to want to pay special attention to him. He could look as good as anyone in the history of mankind, but it wouldn't matter at all. Everyone in town seemed to think they knew what had happened and had made up their own minds. Dante wasn't going to change them, so he stayed away.

"I need to go to Paris and London for business in the next few weeks. Could you please arrange the travel for me? I left the dates on my desk." After tonight, he'd wrap up the business he needed to in St. Giles and escape to Europe for a while. He had plenty of business to attend to, and he was always happier over there. He had friends there who knew nothing of his past, and that was exactly how he liked it.

"Of course." Roberts handed him a set of keys. "The car is out front. Now, have a good time and do what you need to." He brushed what Dante figured was imaginary lint off Dante's shoulders and then stepped aside.

"Thank you." Dante left his room and descended the stairs of the house where three generations of his family had lived. As a kid, he'd loved this place, with its rich woodwork and the paintings and sculptures his mother had collected throughout her life. Now it was a showplace… for one. Well, that and the people who worked for him. Others rarely saw it, and even then got no farther than the hall and his office. He'd closed up much of the rest of the house. Why have the staff clean rooms that were never used and weren't likely to be used again? Well, not in his lifetime anyway, and who knew who'd live here after he was gone. It wasn't as though he'd ever have children, much to his late father's chagrin.

Dante walked out of the house to the midnight-blue BMW that sat right out front. Its top was already down, and he stopped and took a deep breath. He could do this; it was only a car. Dante slid behind the wheel and turned over the engine, which purred to life. He'd forgotten what it felt like to experience this car, and Dante put it into gear and glided out of the drive and down the hill toward the town, the clean, refreshing night air clearing some of the cobwebs from his head.

He turned at the main stoplight in town, then continued out to the Community Center to the north. The Foundation had built the building under his father's tenure, and shit and blast if it didn't have their fucking name in big letters on the side. As soon as he saw it as he pulled into the lot, Dante gripped the wheel tight. He was directed to a spot right up front, and after putting up the top, he made a call. "Yates. Are you at this fundraiser yet?"

"Of course."

"Then you saw the side of the building?" he gritted through his teeth.

"Of course."

"I want you to have those damn letters removed and rename the place the St. Giles Community Center. My father might have liked everyone knowing every stupid little thing he did in perpetuity, but that ends. Can you do that for me, and as soon as possible?" He ended the call without waiting for an answer and got out of the car. Taking a deep breath, he walked toward the entrance, which was festooned with arches of fairy lights wound through white flowers. He smiled when he saw it, remembering that his mother loved white roses.

A few people congregated outside, talking. They turned toward him, the women with a look of surprise as their conversations stopped, and then they all moved out of the way so he could pass. He half expected them to curtsey or something, except for the shock and fear in their eyes. He ignored it, went inside the building, and stepped into the foyer, which had been decorated with more arches. Waiters in white shirts weaved through the crowd, all decked out in their finest, the conversations swirling through the room like a trapped fog that wasn't able to dissipate or escape.

There was a wave of silence as the collective talking came to a stop and all heads turned toward him at the same time. One of the waiters approached, and Dante took a glass of champagne from the tray, thanked him, and continued on through the room. He'd known it would be like this and had been stupid to even bother coming. The town rumor mill had had plenty to feed itself on over the years, and it seemed the stories had gotten bigger with each retelling.

"It will be all right," Yates said as he came up and stood next to him.

"Do you think I care what these people think?" Dante asked, then drank, emptying half the glass. "God, this stuff is awful." He set the glass on a nearby tray. "Is there a bar?" He hoped so. Maybe two or three double whiskies would do the trick.

"Yes. It's in the room off to the side over there."

Yates seemed exasperated as Dante stomped off to get himself something that would make this night tolerable. There was a line, but it evaporated when people saw him, and he practically walked up to the bar. He ordered and paid for his drinks, placed a nice tip in the jar, and left the room before the whispers could start. For two years he'd stayed away, putting on a brave front, but…. Dante raised the glass to his lips, downed the first of his scotches, and set the glass aside. He held the second one, intending to sip it for a while.

The waves of people seemed to part, and Dante got a glimpse of a brown-haired man with intense blue eyes standing on the other side of the room. His nose was crooked and he was a little gawky. Handsome wasn't a word that Dante would have used to describe him. He had seen better-looking men, but few with the intensity and drive that churned in those blue orbs. His tuxedo looked at least one size too big for him, and his shirt was a little wrinkled. Dante barely noticed. What he saw were those fiery eyes and a pair of lips turned up in a smile as he spoke to the short lady in front of him. Dante had seen plenty of beautiful people, but few of them captured his attention the way this man did.

"Yates," Dante said as his lawyer passed nearby, tugging him off his path. "Who is he?" Dante didn't dare take his gaze off him for fear that he was an illusion and would disappear into the crowd and Dante would never see him again.

"Beau Clarity. He runs one of the programs at the Center. That's the reason for tonight's fundraiser. We're expanding counseling services here, and he runs the program." Yates brushed something off Dante's arm.

"How is that possible? He looks like…." Words escaped him. An angel, or maybe it was the devil himself in an ill-fitting suit but with a nose and face that stopped Dante in his tracks. Beau chuckled and then laughed, adding to the glitter of the evening with the joy in his eyes.

"I've only met him briefly. It's my understanding that he's somewhat older than he looks. Granted, at my age, all of you look like children. He's got a master's degree in counseling, and from all I've heard, he's very gifted." Yates excused himself as everyone was ushered into the large community room, which had been transformed into a garden of delight with flowers of every description.

The sweet scent filled Dante's nose, and everywhere he looked there was color, something to delight the eyes. Even the beams overhead that supported the room, utilitarian as they were, had been transformed into a magical canopy with vines and lights. He nearly walked into one of the tables, he was so fascinated with what was around him.

Others seemed to be finding their tables, but Dante wasn't sure where he was expected to sit, if anyone had actually been expecting him to show up at all.

"Mr. Bartholomew?" a young boy of about eight said in a soft voice. "I was asked to show you to your table." He raised his hand, and Dante hesitated before taking it, letting the child lead him through throngs of people as chairs slid along the floor and a crush of conversation and movement nearly drowned out the thoughts in his head. "Mr. Clarity said you were supposed to sit here." He smiled, pointing to a seat.

Dante knelt down. "What's your name?" he asked, paying little attention to the people moving around him.

A man tried to pass and stumbled as he bumped into him. "You should look what you're—" His words cut off abruptly as Dante drew himself up. Surprise and fear warred with each other, and the man turned and headed off the other way without another word. Dante shook his head and turned his attention back to his young escort, kneeling down once again.

"I'm Bobby, and I'm supposed to sit next to you." He pulled out his chair and climbed onto it, then sat upright, looking completely uncomfortable, and Dante wondered if he'd been instructed on exactly how he was to behave tonight. "They had a contest at school and I won, so I got to come, and then Mr. Clarity asked me if I would stay with you and look after you."

"I see. Well, you've done a good job." Dante smiled and looked up as others joined him. They all seemed a little unsure.

"Mr. Clarity," Bobby said as the stunning man Dante had seen earlier approached. "Did I do okay?"

"Yes. You did great." He patted Bobby on his shoulder and then raised his intense gaze to Dante. "Beau Clarity." He extended his hand.

"Dante Bartholomew."

"It's good to meet you, Mr. Bartholomew." They shook hands. Beau's grip was firm and dry.

"Dante, please." They both sat down as servers spread throughout the room with the first courses. "Have you been here in town very long?" he asked, needing to say something. The others at the table were talking among themselves, including Mayor Grant and his wife. He was nice enough, Dante supposed, but his wife always looked like she'd been sucking on a lemon and couldn't find her lips any longer.

"About six months. The Center wanted to offer counseling for people who were trying to end their substance abuse, so I applied. They helped me move here and even found me a place to live." Beau smiled at him, and suddenly, even with the air-conditioning turned all the way to winter, Dante seemed extra warm. He drank most of his water and did his best not to pull at his collar.

"That's good. I'm glad the Foundation was able to help."

A throat clearing on the other side of him drew his attention, and he turned to Mayor Grant.

"We've put forward a city beautification project that we were wondering if the Bartholomew Foundation would like to undertake."

Dante stifled a huff. "What sort of project?"

"We wanted to acquire large stone planters for the main street to fill with flowers and greenery." Mayor Grant smiled and showed Dante a picture of what he had in mind.

"Who will maintain them?" Date asked, knowing the answer already. "The same people who don't maintain the play area at River Rock Park, or the people who've let city hall deteriorate to the point that you want to build a new one?" Dante leaned closer. "I suggest you figure out how you are going to improve and maintain what you have." He met the mayor's steely gaze with one of his

10

own, baring his teeth slightly. "Better yet, I understand you're going to run for another term. I suggest we need some new blood. You obviously aren't up to the task." He watched as Mayor Grant turned completely white, and his wife leaned forward.

"How dare you…!" she sputtered.

"I'm a citizen like anyone else, and I'm entitled to my opinion. Besides, I certainly didn't vote for your husband." He turned away as Jerry Hansen, the most likely mayoral challenger, grinned to beat the band. "Whoever does the job is going to have to learn to live within their own budget and do what is best for the entire town, not just their own hardware store." He shot another glare at Mayor Grant, whom he'd always thought of as useless. Dante and the Bartholomew Foundation provided a great deal for the town, but over the years, the town had come to rely on it for everything and had forgotten their own stewardship, at least in Dante's opinion, and that was going to end.

Dante turned back to Bobby. "Do you know what we're going to have for dinner?"

"Roast beef and potatoes and beans." Bobby made a face. "I don't like beans."

"Bobby," Beau said gently.

"Why not? They're good, and they make you grow up big and strong. My mom always made me eat my green beans, and look at me." Dante sat up straight, and Bobby's eyes widened.

"These are green and yellow beans together," Beau clarified.

"Even better. The yellow ones make you smarter. I really like those. And it's good to be smart." Dante nudged Bobby. "I'll make a deal with you. If you eat all your beans, then after dinner, I'll see if they have any ice cream for dessert."

Bobby shook his head. "There's cake." He pushed out his lower lip. "I can't have cake. It has gluten in it." He turned away, his little shoulders drooping.

"I see." Dante pulled out his phone and made a very quick call to Harriet at the house, then began to eat. When he was done with his starter, his salad was placed in front of him, and he ate it slowly. The lady from the other couple, who had been quiet so far, asked him about what the Foundation did. "It's to better the people and community of St. Giles and Maryland in general, though we localize our work to the Eastern Shore. We take proposals from anyone and evaluate them for community impact and need."

"Do you get anything out of it?" she asked.

"I own the porcelain works, and half the profits go into the Foundation. We invest the money and then arrange to distribute the earnings through our projects. The principal is never touched, and so far it has grown each year through contributions." Dante finished his salad and glanced at Bobby, who was carefully eating one piece of lettuce at a time.

"I'm Clyde Harrison, and this is my wife, Jean. I'm a second-shift foreman at the porcelain works." He reached across the table to shake hands, and Jean did the same. They both seemed nervous, like if they said one wrong thing, Dante would fire him.

"It's nice to meet you, Jean." He turned to Clyde. "I've seen you at the plant." He thought for a second. "You were the one who came up with the idea to reroute the laboratory-ware line last year. That was a great idea, and it'll be done next month. We figure it will save us quite a bit." Dante had already arranged a bonus for him, but he'd let that work through the channels.

The conversation died, and Dante turned to Bobby, who had eaten about half his salad and seemed to be finished. "Are you done?" Dante asked him, and Bobby nodded. The servers collected their plates and brought the dinners.

"Do I have to eat all this?" Bobby whispered. "Mama says I have to clean my plate and not waste food." He looked at him and then at Beau.

"Just eat what you want and have some of the beans." Dante winked, and Bobby took a bite of the beans and ate a few before starting on the rest. Beau helped Bobby cut his meat, and then the kid ate like a trooper. "Is it good?" Dante asked.

Bobby grinned, nodded, and went back to eating. Dante took a few bites and ate a little of the roast beef. It was okay. The potatoes weren't exceptional. He ate the vegetables and enough of the rest to make his hunger abate and then waited for his plate to be cleared.

As the conversation in the room increased while the courses were changed, Dante excused himself and left the room. Roberts stood waiting for him. "Harriet added some ice to make sure this stayed cold."

"Thank you." Dante took the small cooler bag and carried it back into the banquet room. Pieces of cake had been distributed, with one sitting in front of each place, including Bobby's, taunting the poor kid. Dante moved the cake aside and opened the bag. He took out a bowl of Harriet's homemade chocolate ice cream and set it at Bobby's place. "Guaranteed gluten-free."

"Thank you!" Bobby said and began to eat like he hadn't just had dinner.

"Ladies and gentlemen," Yates said after taking the dais. "We want to thank each of you for coming tonight and supporting the St. Giles Community Rehabilitation Clinic. This is a relatively new service that we are pleased to offer, and with your ongoing support, this program will continue well into the future." Everyone clapped politely. "I'd especially like to thank Dante Bartholomew and the Bartholomew Family Foundation for their donation of the first $50,000 of our fundraising efforts. They agreed to match the first $50,000 in donations, and I'm pleased to report that as of tonight we have surpassed that goal, thanks to all of you." The applause grew more intense. "Now, I'd like to bring up Beau Clarity to tell you a little about the programs offered and what you're helping bring to the community."

The applause rang out, and Beau stepped up on the small stage to stand behind the podium.

"I want to welcome you all here tonight. You are supporting programs that help people with substance-abuse issues deal with their problems so they can return to leading productive lives. Alcoholism and substance abuse don't just affect the user—they affect us all. Their families, coworkers, and everyone else in their lives. Tonight, through your generous donations, you are helping families come back together and helping to heal wounds that would otherwise tear people apart. So I want to thank each and every one of you for your generosity, and especially Dante Bartholomew, who has joined us here this evening." Beau motioned to where Dante sat. "I'd also like to ask one more thing. Supporting the clinic financially is wonderful and we appreciate it, but volunteering and becoming part of our programs is equally appreciated. We have plenty of opportunities, and we are grateful for all the help we can get. Thank you." Beau stepped down and took his seat once again.

Dante ate his rubbery cake and kept to himself, checking his watch and wondering how soon he could go home. The rumor mill had taken a break so far, but he could see people looking at him and talking. Dante wanted to tell them to mind their own business, but it wasn't going to do any good.

Bobby had finished his ice cream and left the table to join the few other kids in the corner, where one of the adults seemed to be organizing them for something.

"We could really use your help," Beau told him. "I know you give plenty of money, but some of your time with kids who come in for therapy would be wonderful. Substance abuse affects the entire family."

Dante felt himself pale. "No." He managed not to scream the word and checked his watch yet again. It was way past time to get the hell out of here and back to his quiet house. He'd done what they wanted and put in an appearance. He'd been nice. Of course, he'd also told off the mayor, but that was just the cherry on top of the evening. "I am very busy. But I am pleased the Foundation was able to support your good work."

Dante was about to make his getaway when the group of kids filed onto the stage.

"Mr. Bartholomew," Bobby said, holding out his hand.

Dante stood and walked up to them, and Beau joined them on the dais.

"The children were told about your matching gift to the Center, and they made you something." Beau smiled, and each of the kids likewise had a huge grin. Beau stepped to the back of the stage and brought out a gold-framed drawing. "Each of the kids drew a picture of themselves, and we had the drawing framed for you."

Everyone applauded, and Dante took the colored pencil drawing framed in gold-painted macaroni. "This is very special. Thank you all so much." He didn't know what else to say as six small, grinning faces looked back at him. "I'll put this up in my office so I can see it every day."

They filed off the stage, and Dante carried the frame back to his seat. He set it on the table and got a drink from a passing waiter. He downed the scotch and then picked up the frame before finding Yates and saying good night.

He had never been so happy to slide into his car in his life. He placed the frame on the back seat and drove home as quickly as possible, pulled the car in front of the house, and went inside.

"How did it go?" Roberts asked.

Dante took off his tie and jacket and handed them to him before going into his office and closing the door. Sometimes life really sucked. Not that he didn't deserve whatever cold shoulder and whispered conversations he got. He poured a large glass of scotch from the bottle in the cabinet near his desk, sat back in his chair, and figured tonight was a good night to get drunk.

A knock on the door halted the glass on its trip to his lips. "I had the car put around in the garage, and this picture was on the back seat."

"The children gave it to me tonight, and I told them I'd put it up in my office." Dante drank half the glass of scotch, the liquid slipping smoothly down his throat. He waved his hand. "Just find an appropriate place for it." He waved his hand once again, and Roberts left the room. Dante poured himself another glass and did his best not to let images of the intensely attractive Beau Clarity run though his mind like a parade of horniness. The man was something else, and maybe with enough to drink, his smooth voice and the fire in his eyes would abate and Dante would be able to forget them.

DANTE SAT at his desk, looking up from his work and right at the framed picture the kids had given him. Every time he took a break, there it was. When he'd told Roberts to find an appropriate place to hang it, he hadn't really meant on his office wall right in front of him, where he saw it every time he looked up.

For the last two weeks, he'd seen it and even stopped to gaze at the children's drawings of themselves, and damn it all if he didn't think of Beau and his intense eyes every time. Beau wasn't handsome, or even generally good-looking in a conventional way, but he had spirit and fire and was willing to let them show. Dante had done his best to bury himself in work and in the preparations for his upcoming trip to Europe. He'd originally planned to leave in a week, but orders and the work they'd need to do at the plant to fill them had delayed his trip. So instead of going to London first, he'd moved that stop to last and kept the rest of his itinerary intact.

Roberts knocked and then entered Dante's office with a tray. He set a cup of coffee on the edge of the desk, along with a plate of cookies. They were the oddest-looking cookies he'd ever seen, more oblong than round, and a little lumpy.

"Did Harriet make these?" If she had, he'd begin to wonder if she was starting to slip.

"No. These were sent to you from the children." Roberts pointed to the drawing on the wall. "Apparently you were nice to one of them at the dinner and he wanted to say thank you. He and his friends baked some cookies for you, and Mr. Clarity had them sent over." Roberts left the office, and Dante picked up a cookie and took a small bite. They were good, if a little dry, but nice with the coffee.

He looked up and saw the picture. "Roberts…," Dante called, and his office door opened, Roberts entering once again. "Please call the Community Center and tell Mr. Clarity that I'd be willing to volunteer… say, on an afternoon or evening later this week, to help out." Dante smiled because he knew that somehow Roberts had a hand in this. "In fact, we're all going to volunteer, including Harriet." Misery loved company, after all.

"Very good, sir. I'll make the phone calls and schedule it." Roberts turned and left the office.

Dante went back to work, strangely excited about seeing Beau again. He wasn't sure if this was a good idea or one of the stupidest notions ever conceived. But it would make Yates happy. Yes, that was it. He was doing this to help improve his image in the community.

Dante told himself that over and over all afternoon in the hope that he'd eventually come to believe it, but he wasn't sure it worked.

CHAPTER 2

"YOU'VE GOT to be kidding me!" Angie said after Beau got off the phone and told her about his conversation. "The Beast of St. Giles is going to come here to volunteer some of his time?" She shuddered, and he had a feeling it wasn't for dramatic effect. "There is no way you can allow that. And he's going to work with the kids? He'll have those sweet little things traumatized beyond all recognition."

"He was great with them at the dinner. Bobby likes him and even sent him cookies." Beau stepped to the desk where she was handling some of the mountains of paperwork that helped keep them funded. Angie had great skill in getting money out of turnips… and everyone else.

She gasped. "You've only been here a few months, so you probably haven't heard what he did. He was married, and his wife died… let me see… almost three years ago. People say they were never in love and only married because his father forced him to just to get his inheritance, and after he got it, they say he killed her. The authorities investigated, but he had too much money and influence… and got off." The last part was hissed under her breath.

"You believe these rumors?" Beau looked down his nose.

"I don't know. Sometimes rumor is a bunch of hogwash, but often there's a nugget of truth that started it. The thing is, I don't want to be the one to find out." She turned back to her computer. "Just let me know when he's going to be here so I can work from home." With that pronouncement she returned to her work.

Beau didn't know what to say. He had no facts to back the rumors up, but other than probably wanting to be alone and not the target of rumor and speculation, he hadn't seen anything in Dante that he read as beastly. Well, other than putting the mayor in his place, which from what he'd heard wasn't necessarily a bad thing.

"Angie…." He hardened his gaze until she looked up at him.

"What?" she snapped.

"This is a crisis and counseling center. We help everyone, and if Dante Bartholomew is willing to give of his time for us, then we're going to take it and make sure he feels welcome." He leaned over the desk. "That means treating him like we do the rest of our volunteers. Apparently he also gave his entire household staff the day off so they could help us here as well."

She rolled her eyes. "Yeah, the Beast got his own people to help us."

Beau shook his head and held his temper, taking a deep breath. "Dante is going to try to help us. He gives plenty to support our work." He saw he wasn't getting through, so he changed tack. "What if the rumors are wrong? You never impressed me as the kind of person who judged people based on talk. You help everyone here, and you're going to turn your back on him?"

"Dang you…," she muttered and then groaned. "Fine. I'll be nice to him."

"Just treat him like you would anyone else. You don't need to treat him special."

She nodded. "But if he's mean to any of the kids, or to me, so help me…."

"I don't think you need to worry about him being mean to anyone, unless it's the mayor. Then it's no holds barred." He had to smile, and Angie pursed her lips.

"That little nugget was all over town in five minutes. I wish I'd have been there to see him put that old goat and his lemon-sucking wife in their place." She sighed once again, mirth filling her eyes. "Okay. I'll give him a chance…." She held up her index finger. "One."

Smiling, Beau left her to get back to work while he went to find his group of kids.

One of the programs he'd instituted since coming here was for families. Addiction affected more than the addict. Their spouses, children, and parents all suffered in one form or another. His biggest success had been with the youngsters. Beau had set up one room in the facility specifically for them, with bulletin boards, brightly colored walls, and puzzle-square carpet. He wanted kids to feel comfortable in the space when he met with them. Beau worked with the school and parents to help these kids get the support they needed. He only had them a few times a week for a couple of hours, but he loved his work and wouldn't trade it for anything.

"Mr. Beau," Bobby called as he entered the room. Bobby hurried over and Beau knelt down for a hug, then got one from each of the kids in turn. "Did he get the cookies we made?"

"Yes, he did, and I'm told he liked them." Beau leaned close. "He's going to come in for our next meeting and help out. So you all need to be nice to him."

"He's a beast," Kendra said, her arms folded over her chest. "My mommy said so."

"You're just a goody-two-shoes know-it-all," Hank told her, then stuck out his tongue.

"That's enough of that," Beau said gently, even though he agreed with Hank. Kendra thought she knew everything about everything, and whatever her mother said might as well have been a pronouncement from God. "You don't need to come next time if you don't want to, but Mr. Bartholomew is going to help us."

"Will he bring ice cream?" Bobby asked. That was why Beau loved these kids so much. There was little guile in them. They said what they were thinking and what they wanted.

"I don't know. But that isn't why he's coming." Beau stood and got the kids into a circle. Most of their time together was playtime, with him asking a few questions. He had to tread carefully, as some of these kids were still half scared of their own shadows. When the kids first came to him, they were aggressive and misbehaved a lot. Kendra was the newest addition to the group, but her acting out

20

took the form of always having to be right. It was annoying, but she was getting better, right along with her mother.

"But he's mean," Kendra said softly.

"Has he ever been mean to you?" Beau asked, then waited while she muttered her answer and lowered her arms in defeat. "We should listen to Mommy and Daddy, but it's also okay to make up your own mind about people." He smiled, and Kendra gave him a tiny grin. "Now, let's do something."

"I want to make a picture for Mr. Dante," Bobby said before rushing over to the table with the tub of colored pencils. Beau got him some paper while the others decided what they wanted to do. Some of the kids liked to play on their own. Bobby was one of those. His father had become addicted to painkillers after back surgery, and at times he'd gotten aggressive when he needed the pills he didn't have.

"How is your dad?" Beau asked, sitting next to Bobby once Angie came in and started the others in a game of duck, duck, goose.

Bobby nodded but didn't answer right away. "He scares me," he finally answered without looking away from his picture.

"Is he angry, like before?" Beau hoped he wasn't using again. It was a constant threat for these kids. Just when things got better for them... they rode a roller coaster of sobriety and relapse.

"No." Bobby continued coloring and then put down his pencil. He turned, lower lip quivering, tears pooling in his eyes. "Daddy says he wants to get married... and not to Mommy. Kendra says that means I'm going to have an evil stepmother like Cinderella did." He threw his arms around Beau's neck and held him tight. "I don't wanna have an evil stepmother."

There were times when Beau wanted to laugh. He knew he couldn't, though. "Have you met the lady your daddy wants to marry?" When Bobby nodded against his shirt, he asked, "Is she nice?"

"She made me gluten-free cookies. She said she's a nurse at the hospital." Bobby sniffled, wiping his nose with his hand.

"If she's nice, then she can't be evil. She'll be your stepmother, yes. But she doesn't sound like she's evil to me." Sometimes kids, especially the ones who had seen true hardship, took stories too much to heart.

"But what if she turns evil? She isn't a stepmother yet." He pulled back a little to rub his eyes.

"I don't think she's going to turn evil. Does she spend time with you and your dad?" Beau asked, and Bobby nodded. "Do you like her?"

"She's nice. She took me on a bike ride. We raced and I won. She laughed and said I was going to grow up strong like my daddy." Bobby blinked.

"Then I think she's going to be a good stepmother. I had one of those."

"You did?" Bobby asked as though he'd never thought about it.

"I did. My mommy died when I was your age, and my daddy got married again. Her name is Rose and I love her like she was my mother." Beau had been very lucky in that regard. "No evil at all. Though she did take away my NES when I was naughty, but she always gave it back. She's a very nice lady, and it sounds like yours is going to be too. Why don't you draw a picture for her?" He gently held Bobby until he moved out of his arms and went back to drawing.

"Is he okay?" Angie asked once Beau left Bobby to his task and the kids were playing their game.

Beau nodded and sighed. Dealing with the emotional load the kids couldn't was sometimes the most difficult part of his job. These kids were innocents, affected by the actions of others. "How is the game?"

"Fine, though they're going to get tired of it soon."

"Then let's have them color on their own. We can ask each of them to draw a picture of their mother or father. Sometimes those pictures can tell us a lot about what's going on in their heads. Words can be hard for them, but they can and do express themselves."

Beau got things ready while Angie ended the game, and then the kids came to the tables. They set to work, and Beau talked to each one in turn, asking them how they were doing and getting hugs, sometimes drying tears, especially from Kendra, who was a bundle of nerves and fear once he got under her façade.

By the time the morning was over and the kids had been picked up, Beau was exhausted. He slumped behind his desk in his tiny private office to clear his email and see to what else needed to be done. The benefit a few weeks earlier had brought a nice influx of cash, and the drive continued to bring in donations. So at least for now, they were doing fairly well, though just barely staying on budget.

A knock pulled him out of his review of the Center's finances. "It's open." He set the spreadsheet printout aside and smiled as an older gentleman came in. "May I help you?"

"Hello. I'm Roberts. I work for Mr. Bartholomew."

"Yes, I talked to you on the phone." Beau kept his smile in place. "Is there something I can help you with?" He motioned to a chair, and Roberts sat down slowly.

"We are set to volunteer in a few days, and I thought it best to see you and determine if there was anything that you'd like us to bring or provide." He tugged his suit coat until it was completely wrinkle-free. It made Beau feel underdressed in his red polo shirt and khaki pants.

"You don't need to bring anything. We appreciate you being generous with your time." Beau stood and walked to the door to close it. "I get the feeling there's something you want to talk about."

Roberts nodded. "I know the rumors that float around town. I hear them—we all do. But I don't believe any of them."

Beau nodded carefully. "I don't put much faith in rumor either, though it seems most of the town does." He gathered his papers into a small pile to clean up his messy desk. "Were you here when the incidents that seem to be the source of the rumors happened?"

"No. Mr. Bartholomew's father passed away a little over three years ago, just before the incidents, though his father's passing does figure into some of the rumors. I came to work for Mr. Bartholomew after his father died."

"What is it you're trying to say?" Beau asked, furrowing his brow.

"I'm asking that you give him a chance." There was genuine affection in Robert's eyes, and that sat very well with Beau. If he could engender such loyalty from the people who worked directly with him, then that told Beau a great deal about the man himself.

"Mr. Bartholomew is coming here to volunteer and to give of himself. That is something I always appreciate. Some of our programs wouldn't exist if it weren't for the countless volunteer hours given generously and selflessly. I appreciate Mr. Bartholomew agreeing to volunteer." Beau was beginning to wonder just what he was getting himself into. Never in his life had so much fuss been made over one person's choice to spend a few hours at the Center. Heck, he was starting to wonder if a presidential or royal visit warranted this much fuss.

"Thank you." Roberts stood, and Beau followed suit. "Mr. Bartholomew wanted me to ask if the children will be here the day he's coming."

"Yes. I thought he'd work with them. He seemed to hit it off with Bobby at the dinner, and Bobby's been asking about him."

"Excellent. Thank you." Roberts left the office, and Beau closed the door after him, wondering what in the heck all that was about. He didn't have much time, though; his next appointment was in ten minutes, and he needed a chance to get ready.

The rest of the day was one appointment or group session after another. The demands on the Center had continued to grow since his arrival because of an increase in various street drugs. Beau was exhausted by the time he left the Center, well after most people had had dinner. He stopped at a diner to pick up an order he'd called in and took it home to the apartment the Center provided for him just two blocks away.

He trudged up the stairs and inside the one-bedroom, three-room place. He had a small living room, kitchen, and bedroom, plus a large bathroom, which made the apartment worth all its other challenges. He locked the door, grabbed a bottle of water from the mostly empty refrigerator, and sat on the sofa to eat his club sandwich and salad.

He'd just finished his salad and was unwrapping his sandwich when his phone rang. "Hi," he said brightly when he answered.

"Are you okay? You haven't called in a while, and your father was worried." That was his stepmother's code for she was worried and had to call.

"I'm just fine. Been really busy, too busy, since the fundraiser." Which they had attended. "I'm getting plenty of volunteers, including the town's most elusive citizen."

She gasped. "You mean that beast man? Everyone at the dinner was talking about him. He apparently killed his wife because he got tired of her, so he wouldn't have to give her half of what he has in a divorce." She clicked her lips. "You be careful of that man. I didn't like the look of him."

That was strange, because Dante Bartholomew was more than easy on the eyes. "You have to be kidding…. He's take-me-out-and-shoot-me gorgeous, and you know it." Dark hair and eyes as deep as the earth, rich olive skin that gave him a touch of the dreamy, and a body that could only be hinted at under those clothes.

"You are not allowed to be smitten with him."

"Smitten?" Beau laughed. "I love your words sometimes." She read a lot, mainly mysteries, and right now she must be reading Victorian stories of intrigue and drawing rooms. "No, I'm not smitten, and I don't like it when people call others names." He cleared his throat. "His family foundation gave enough in that one night to pay my salary for the next year."

"I'm just saying—"

"That you listened to idle gossip," he said, giving her a little dose of guilt.

"Where there's smoke, there's fire," she countered. "And everyone was talking about it. I heard the story from three different people."

"That may be, but I saw something else." Beau couldn't say quite what it was. He'd only been with Dante for a few hours, but he didn't see a killer in those eyes. He'd seemed shy and hadn't talked to many people at all. It was clear Dante had a temper, especially with the way he took on the mayor, but most of the night he'd been quiet and rather withdrawn. Maybe still waters ran deep—and in this case, dangerous—but Beau's gut told him there was something else going on.

"I see. Is that your professional opinion?" she snipped at him.

"Nope. But it is mine and I'm allowed to have it." He grinned. "Oh, I have to tell you. I used you as an example today." He relayed the crux of what Bobby had said without telling her his name or getting into much detail.

"I'm glad I'm not in the evil category." She chuckled. "Downright relieved, as a matter of fact."

"Me too." Beau sat back, looking longingly at his dinner. "I need to finish eating."

"All right, honey. Call us when you get a chance."

She hung up, and Beau put the phone on the table, instantly wishing he'd kept talking to her. The apartment was quiet, lonely, and didn't yet feel like home. This wasn't his first job, but it had taken him far enough away that it felt like it. He turned on the television and ate his sandwich. Once he was done, he took care of the paper and dishes before settling on the sofa to watch a movie, but dropped off to sleep well before it was time for him to go to bed.

THE DAYS slipped by in a whirl of activity, and Beau had no idea why he was nervous. People were volunteering to help, which happened all the time, but for some reason, he was keyed up about Dante coming in.

"Settle down. This isn't a visit from His Holiness." Angie sat at her desk, doing her normal work. "Do you like this guy or something?" She made an *ewww* face as soon as she said the words.

"Look, I don't care how dreamy he looks. You are not allowed to… whatever… God, don't make me say it… just no!"

Beau grinned. "So you think he's dreamy?" he teased just so he could watch Angie get all red in the face.

"That's what you took away from that?" She looked on the verge of having a fit. Beau had to stop himself from laughing.

"It's what you said." He sighed dramatically. "And you're right. He is dreamy and I wonder…. Those tuxedos hide everything… but…." He fanned himself, and Angie sprang to her feet.

"You are not allowed to…." She glared at him. "You meanie, pain in the ass! You are so not allowed to tease me like that." She waved her finger at him, and Beau grinned like an idiot. At the very least, his nervousness was gone.

"Come on. Give me some credit. I don't even know the man, other than talking to him for a little while." Besides, he wasn't going to go into the fact that Dante Bartholomew obviously traveled quite a bit and met a ton of people. He could have any good-looking man he wanted, as long as they weren't from St. Giles, apparently. Why would he be interested in someone as plain and… well…. Beau pushed the thought from his head. He didn't need to go into his issues at the moment. And he certainly wasn't going to be showing them to Dante. "Besides, I never said anything about being interested in him other than having him help here at the Center. The rest of it was all on you."

Angie cocked her grin just a little. "It's a gift." She winked.

"I've heard it called many things, but never that." He folded his arms over his chest.

"A dirty mind is a terrible thing to waste." She turned away, then quickly spun back. "And speak of the devil," she whispered, the smile falling from her lips as Dante entered the building through the front doors and approached the desk rather hesitantly.

"Hello," Beau said. "I'm Beau. We talked at the dinner."

"I remember." Dante shook his hand. "Do I need to sign in or something?"

Angie handed him a form, and Dante filled it out, signed it, and handed it back.

"I've never done this sort of thing before. What do you want me to do?"

"Well, Bobby has been asking about you." Beau motioned down the hall, then paused. "Actually, he keeps asking if you're going to bring ice cream with you."

"Harriet will be over in half an hour, and I'm told she made an entire batch to share. I expect that everyone in the Center will probably go into a sugar coma by the time she's done." Dante smiled, and danged if he didn't light up. His teeth were perfectly white and his smile was infectious, making Beau smile as well.

"We're right down here," he said, leading Dante to the room. "The kids will come here in a few minutes, and they stay for a couple of hours. I talk to each of them to see how things are with them, and if you can organize some games and activities with them, that would be great."

"What games? What sort of things do they like? I don't know any games."

"They like to color, and there are plenty of board games that will work. Just be yourself." Beau felt sorry for the guy; he looked lost. "These are kids who have had a hard time of it already. Their parent or parents have substance-abuse issues. Some of them have mixed feelings about their parents. They love them, but they hate them too because of what they've done."

"Okay." Dante appeared ready to bolt, his gaze darting around the room.

"Just be caring and thoughtful. You don't need to talk about anything other than what you're doing. This is a safe place for them. If one of them starts to cry, be caring and understanding. Sometimes something innocent will trigger a response from them. It isn't your fault if it happens." Beau walked to a plastic tub and pulled off the lid. "You can start with this if you'd like. There are

28

thousands of Lego blocks. Think of something fun and ask them to make it. Use your imagination."

"All right."

"I'm going to be here with you, so you have nothing to worry about. Have some fun." Beau smiled.

"What about Roberts and the others?"

"Angie will be working with them. There is so much we could use help with, and she's the queen of organization."

Dante chuckled. "Wait till she meets Roberts. He's the king." Dante picked through the blocks and began absently putting them together.

"Do you have any questions?" Beau asked, catching Dante's gaze. Heat sprang up inside, and a slight sheen of sweat broke out on the back of his neck. He turned away and took a deep breath. When he turned back, Dante was still looking at him. Beau cleared his throat to try to speak, but his voice didn't work. Being the subject of that gaze was completely unexpected. Beau had seen heat and lust in people before. He knew what they looked like, and that look had both but something else as well—longing and fear. Beau was well acquainted with both of those as well. Within seconds they disappeared, replaced with the same steely cold Beau had seen while Dante had been talking to the mayor.

"No. I can work with the kids." Blinking and remaining stern, he turned to where the kids would sit in their small group, taking in the space again.

"Mr. Beau!" Bobby called as he raced into the room, followed by Kendra, Hank, Lila, Raymond, and Phillip. They all stopped about three steps in, staring at Dante.

Maybe having Dante come in was a really bad idea. Beau had thought that talking to them last time would smooth the way. This had all the makings of an emotional train wreck.

Bobby hurried to him, gave Beau a hug, and then went right over to Dante. "Did you get the cookies? I had to make them without gluten."

"They were delicious. Thank you." Dante stood still, like he was frozen, and Beau willed him to act the way he had at the dinner.

Bobby tugged on his arm, and Dante finally knelt down. "Did you hang the picture?"

"Yup. Just like I promised. It's in my office."

Bobby whooped and raced back to the other kids. "See?" he said, standing right in front of Kendra, hands on his hips. "I told you he promised."

Beau covered his mouth to keep from laughing. "Why don't you all come over here and say hello to Mr. Dante?"

They approached slowly, especially when Dante stood. The man was huge and had to be intimidating to these small kids.

"He's a giant," Raymond said from the back of the group. "Will he eat us?"

Finally Dante smiled. "I'm not a giant. I'm just tall."

"He looks like a giant." Raymond clearly wasn't going to come any closer.

"Dang," Beau said under his breath. Raymond's father—his estranged father; he now lived with his mother—was as tall as Dante, and he could almost see the triggers going off in the little boy's head. This could be good for him, but only if it became a positive experience, though that possibility seemed to be flying out the door by the second.

"Mr. Beau and I thought it would be fun to play Legos." Dante picked up the container of blocks and dumped it in a pile on the floor. "Can we see who can make the best house?" Dante sat down, and bless Bobby, he plopped right down next to him.

"I want to make a blue house," Bobby said, beginning to pull out all the blue blocks.

"I like the blue ones," Kendra said and joined them, if only to defend her territory.

Hank hurried over and started picking out the white blocks.

"You can make a red house," Dante told Kendra when it seemed she and Bobby were going to get into a fight. "I like the red ones."

Dang it all if Dante didn't smile, and Beau's heart did a little flutter as Kendra backed off for the first time and put the blue blocks she'd been clutching in front of Bobby and began gathering the red ones.

The others hurried over, and soon all of them, except Raymond, who stood next to Beau, holding his hand, his thumb in his mouth, were on the floor, building.

"It's okay. Mr. Dante is nice," Beau told him as gently as he could. Raymond shook his head and moved behind him to try to hide. Beau turned and kept himself between Raymond and Dante. "Is there something you want to tell me about?" Sometimes it was best if he could get them to talk. They didn't always have the words, but sometimes they found them.

Raymond pulled his thumb out of his mouth. "He scares me."

"Why?" Beau asked. "Can you tell me?"

Raymond leaned to the side to look around his legs. "He's big." He looked again and then lifted his gaze. "Where are his horns and big teeth?"

"He's just a person, like you and me." Beau leaned down, gazing over at Dante, who didn't seem at all like any of the rumors he'd heard. Dante turned and looked at him. A zing of heat went right through him. Beau nearly gasped at a moment of sudden insight that hit home when Bobby and Kendra turned to him as well. Each of the kids in the group, no matter how happy they were at the moment, all had that hint of wariness in their eyes, as though they expected the happiness to be short-lived and everything to fall apart once again. He expected to see that with the kids; what he didn't expect was for Dante to have that same darkness. Somehow Dante had been touched by the same pain and hurt as these kids.

"Do you want to go over with me and make a house? We can do it together."

Raymond stared and then nodded slowly.

Beau walked him over, still holding his hand. He considered it a good sign that Raymond didn't put his thumb back in his

31

mouth. They both sat down, everyone making room for them, and Raymond grabbed blocks with one hand, still holding Beau's for a few minutes. Then he pulled away, using both hands to gather the blocks.

"Do you want these?" Dante asked, holding out a few pieces, and Raymond stopped, hesitated, and then nodded. Dante handed them to him. Raymond continued playing but kept looking up at Dante.

What Beau hadn't expected was the way Dante returned Raymond's gaze… with understanding. Somehow Dante knew what these kids were feeling, and Beau wondered how addiction had touched Dante's life. It obviously had somehow.

"Bobby, do you want to talk for a few minutes?" Beau asked, but Bobby shook his head.

"I'm playing with Mr. Dante." Bobby looked at Dante and then returned to his building. Even Kendra, who had been so vocal regarding the Beast at their earlier session, seemed content to play.

"Was your daddy nice?" Bobby asked. It may have seemed like a strange question, but Beau knew it was Bobby's way of asking if Dante's dad was like his dad and the roller coaster of addiction and treatment he'd been through.

"Not really," Dante answered. "My dad…." He paused and then took a look at Beau, who nodded. Being honest with kids was the best way to win them over. "My dad liked to be in control, so when he said something, that was how it was. He didn't like it when I wanted to do things that he didn't want."

"My mommy says I have to do what she says because it's to keep me safe," Raymond volunteered. Beau knew in that second that Dante had won him over.

"Yes. And mommies and daddies want their kids to be safe. But my dad made me get married when I didn't want to."

"Ewww," all the kids said in near unison.

"To a girl." Hank made a yucky face. "I don't want to marry a girl."

"You can marry a boy if you want."

Hank thought about it. "I don't want to marry anyone. But especially not a girl. They're yucky."

"We are not," Kendra immediately countered. "Boys are yucky, not girls."

"Okay," Beau said, bringing an end to the argument. "What Dante means is that if you get married, it should be to someone you love and want to marry. Your dad shouldn't tell you who to marry."

Kendra looked up from where she was concentrating on building the walls of her red house. "Your daddy made you marry someone you didn't want to?" She turned to Beau. "My mommy told me once that she didn't want to marry Daddy, but he made her pregnant with me and she had to marry him." Her hands began to shake, dropping the blocks she held. "She said it was my fault that her life got messed up." Her lower lip quivered, and Beau took her hand to guide her away from the others, then knelt down and hugged her.

"You know that what happened to your mommy isn't your fault." He loved each of these kids and cared deeply about them. They were faultless in their parents' messed-up lives, but sometimes they thought they were to blame for everything that was wrong.

"But what if it was?" she asked, tears streaking down her cheeks.

"It's not. You're a good girl, and what happened to your mommy was never, ever your fault." Sometimes all he could do was reassure these kids. Trying to counter the careless things some parents said was nearly impossible. He let her cry on his shoulder, and once she was done, she went back to building her house.

"Okay. You all finish working on your houses and I'll be right back. The best ones get a treat." Dante stood and worked the kinks out of his legs, then walked over to Beau. "I'm sorry if I said anything that hurt her."

"You didn't. These kids have so many hidden triggers, it's like a minefield sometimes, and hitting them in this environment is safe because I can help them deal with it." Beau smiled. "Go ahead and have fun with them. It's what they need, and believe it

33

or not, you're helping each of them." Beau sat back down and so did Dante.

After working for a while longer, the kids declared their buildings complete.

"You all made such great houses," Dante said, looking at each one.

"Who gets the treat?" Bobby asked, eyes wide.

"Well…." Dante made a show of thinking about it. "How about… all of you?"

"Is it ice cream?" Bobby asked, and Dante's grin was almost as big as Bobby's when he nodded. "Yay! Mr. Dante has the bestest ice cream ever!"

"Harriet arranged to bring some with her. I'm sure if you find her, she'll be able to tell you where it is," Dante said. He certainly knew how to win friends and influence people.

Beau pulled out his phone and called the front desk. Angie answered, and he asked about their treat.

"Harriet will be down in a few minutes. She's in the kitchen area getting things dished up."

"You're one step ahead of me." Beau hung up and told the kids to put their houses on the shelf, then clean up all the remaining blocks and put them in the tub. They moved their creations, which all looked remarkably house-like, and scooped up the blocks.

A woman with her hair pulled into a bun came in carrying a tray. "I hope you all like chocolate," she said gently, and six youngsters all jumped up and down at once.

"Sit at the table," Beau said, and they scrambled into their seats. Harriet handed them each a bowl with a spoon, and they went at it like they were all starving to death. "Thank you," Beau told Harriet and Dante as he watched over his charges.

"The wee ones are adorable," Harriet said with a slight smile. "You just call up to the house and I can make you a batch in no time." She watched them with a grin on her lips.

"Thank you, Harriet. I appreciate all your help," Dante said softly, and once again, Beau wondered about the inconsistencies in this man. If he was such a Beast, why did the kids and the people who worked for him act the way they did?

"They seem so happy," Harriet said, then grabbed some napkins and handed one to each child.

"First and foremost, they're kids," Beau said gently. "They've had harder lives than most...."

Harriet excused herself, saying, "I'll be back for the dishes." She turned. "I have to check on the not-so-wee ones. They're messier." She smiled and left the room.

"She's something else," Beau observed.

"Yes, she is. But do not go anywhere near her kitchen when she's working. She'll bite your head off if you mess up her system." Dante chuckled.

Beau knew it was early in their friendship, but this man was nothing like the one that had been described to him. Where was this Beast that everyone talked about? Kids could tell if someone was inherently mean or bad, and they avoided them. Dante had been generous, thoughtful, and understanding with the kids and with him.

Dante's phone rang and he tugged it out of his pocket. "Is there somewhere I can take this?" When Beau pointed to the door to the small room next door, Dante answered the call and left the room. He spoke quietly into the phone as Beau went to check on the kids.

"Are you almost done?" Beau asked. "If you are, please wipe your hands and face with the napkins and put your bowls and silverware back on the tray. Then you can color for me. Why don't you each draw something that makes you happy?"

They hurried to the tray and took care of the dishes. Beau set them up with paper and colored pencils, and they got busy. Beau then went to check on Dante. He knocked on the door and cracked it open so make sure he was okay.

35

"Fire him!" Dante hissed into the phone. "I want him off the premises today! I will not stand for that in any way." The fire in Dante's voice was freezing enough to send a cold chill up Beau's spine. "You heard me. Right now. Today. Get him gone." Dante stabbed at the phone with his finger, and Beau closed the door and hurried back over to the kids. He checked on their work and watched the door. Dante came out, phone put away, and walked to where the kids were working as though nothing had happened. Beau caught his gaze and couldn't help wondering if he'd just seen the Beast in action.

"What are you drawing?" Dante asked.

"Mr. Beau said to draw what makes us happy." Bobby held up what looked like dish of ice cream. Next to it was a piece of cake that had been crossed out. "Ice cream… not cake."

Dante chuckled. "That's really good. How about you, Kendra?"

"This is my dolly, Brenda. She used to sleep with me every night." Kendra's lower lip quivered. "But when we had to move, she got left behind and…."

"She looks very pretty. What color is her hair?"

"She had black hair like me. She was a Cabbage Patch doll, and I loved her a lot. She kept the monsters away at night. But now she's gone. Mommy says that I'm a big girl now and that I should be able to sleep on my own." Dante appeared to be searching for words to comfort her, but must have come up empty and just hugged her.

Dante asked each of the kids what they were drawing and listened to their answers.

"It's time to go—your parents will be picking you up soon. Put your things away and say goodbye to Mr. Dante." Beau accepted hugs, and so did Dante, each child saying goodbye and Bobby giving Mr. Dante a big hug. Then they filed out, and Beau went through the room, putting everything to rights and cleaning up.

"You did very well," he told Dante, who stood out of the way. "They really liked you."

"They're great kids," Dante said softly. "Is there anything else I can do?"

It was obvious Dante was getting anxious to go. He probably had places he needed to be. "You can go if you like. I appreciate you coming in to spend time with the kids. They need to be exposed to new people, ones who are safe and will help expand their comfort zones." Beau didn't know what else to say. He was curious about this man and wanted to ask him so many questions that he didn't have a right to.

"It was a nice afternoon."

"I'm glad. I hope you'll come back again." Regular volunteers were worth their weight in gold.

"I have to travel in a few weeks, but I will call and arrange to come back." Dante walked toward the door. "This is a really special place...." He put his hand on the knob to leave.

"Maybe you'd like to get together for dinner or something?" Beau almost put his hand over his lips once he realized what he'd said, then backpedaled to try to figure out a way to make what he'd said sound less... needy... less datey. "You give a lot of money to keep programs like this running and I hate to ask for anything more, but I have some ideas, and maybe you could help me plan how to raise the money to make them happen." That sounded pretty good to him. Beau waited for few seconds, sure Dante was going to give him the brush-off.

"I...." Dante paused and then nodded slowly. "Sure. That would be nice." He pulled out his phone. "I have conference calls tomorrow night, but I'm free on Saturday. Why don't you come to the house and we can have dinner and talk? Say, around seven o'clock. Is that okay?"

"Of course." Beau had nothing in particular to do.

"That would be great. I'll see you then." Dante left the room, and Beau wondered what the hell he'd just done.

BEAU SPENT the night thinking of Dante and knew he was in real trouble. All night long he saw those eyes, and more than once he'd woken up jittery and sweaty. Thankfully, the morning came quickly enough, and Beau spent it handling appointments.

He usually packed his lunch, but today he walked down the street to the lunch counter in the department store that had been there since the Roosevelt presidency. The lady behind the counter had probably worked there on opening day. She was kind and knew everyone and everything that happened in town.

"Hi, Beau, honey. You've been gone awhile." She handed him a menu as he perched on one of the old stools with the red leatherette seats.

"I've been really busy and… it's good to see you, Gloria." He smiled. She was one of the first people he'd met when he'd moved to town.

"I hear about the good work you're doing here."

"Thanks."

"I also hear that you had the Beast volunteer yesterday." She caught his gaze. "People here talk about everything."

"That's what I'm counting on." Beau swallowed hard. "I spent hours with him yesterday, and I don't quite get it. I've seen him tear the mayor a new one, and I heard him on the phone with his business, where he sounded as cold as the Arctic. But his staff looks at him like he hung the moon, and he won over all the kids in a matter of minutes. Raymond…."

"Yes. That little boy who was terrorized by his dad." Gloria brought him a Coke and set it in front of him.

"He was scared of Dante, but Dante won Raymond over. I don't get it." Beau was usually so good at reading people, but Dante confused him. Beau purposely kept his own opinions to himself. "Kids know who they trust."

"Yes, they do."

"I was hoping you knew the real story." Beau figured she could shed some light on all this.

"I don't think anyone knows the real story except Dante." The note of sadness in her eyes told him some of what he wanted to know. "As a kid, Dante was always wild and full of energy. He used to come in here and could liven the place up just by walking in the door." She patted Beau's hand gently. "I remember when…." She sighed. "There are some things I know, or at least I think I know. Apparently his father told Dante that in order to get his inheritance, he was going to have to get married, which surprised a lot of us because Dante was gay as far as we all knew. But he married Allison. She was his best friend, and we hoped they could make a go of it. Less than two years later, both Dante's father and his wife were dead. People said she fell down the stairs, and there was a lot of speculation that she was pushed. People stayed away from him, and Dante hasn't left the house very much since, except when he goes out of town. He runs the porcelain works from the house, and we rarely see him. When he is in town, people walk on the other side of the street." Gloria wiped her eyes. "He's surly and rarely talks to anyone."

"Then why did he come to the benefit dinner?" Beau sipped from the glass and set it back down without taking his gaze away from hers.

"Probably because someone told him he had to. Dante hasn't done any of those things since his wife died, and if he volunteered with you, then that's some sort of miracle as well."

"We're having dinner tomorrow at his house, and… I asked him to talk over some new programs for the Center. At least that's what I told him." Beau finally broke her gaze.

She smiled. "You like him." Gloria took his hand in hers. "You know, there's nothing wrong with that, and maybe Dante deserves someone in his life. But be careful. There's a lot of hurt in him, and it's got to come out sometime."

"I…." Beau swallowed really hard. "Was Dante's father… ever abusive… or did he drink… or anything?" Hell, this was hard.

"Hiram? God no. That man never touched a drink of anything in his life. He hated the stuff, and as for anything else…." She

39

shook her head. "The abusive part…." She paused. "I don't like to speak ill of the dead."

"Telling the truth is just that."

"I don't know if he was abusive per se… but he was controlling as all hell. No one in that factory did anything without his say-so. What Hiram wanted, Hiram got, and no one argued with him, including Dante. I mean, what kind of man forces a son to marry someone?"

"Was it because he was gay?" Beau asked, and Gloria grabbed a napkin out of one of the dented aluminum holders to wipe her eyes.

"I think so. Hiram was a closed-minded… know-it-all jerk, to put it in a word. I wouldn't want my worst enemy as his son." She cleared her throat and turned away. "What can I get for you?"

"How about one of your famous BLTs?" Beau asked, trying to process what she'd told him.

Gloria nodded, wrote out a ticket, and placed it on the board for the kitchen. "I know Dante has secrets, plenty of them, and none of us knows what his marriage was like or what happened that night. Only he knows what happened and he's told no one. I doubt he will."

"But why the Beast thing?" Beau asked.

"I don't know. It developed somehow, and then everyone started referring to him that way." A bell sounded, and Gloria went to get his food. "Sometimes things really suck, and maybe all it takes is someone willing to look under the surface to see what's real. Because Lord knows there's a whole lot of speculation, rumor, and storytelling that's embellished this tale to near fairy-tale proportions." She looked down the counter and moved away, filling water glasses as she went.

"That man is a menace," the guy two stools over said as soon as Gloria was out of hearing range. "He gets off on firing people and refuses to listen to anything." The man was probably in his late fifties, half slumped over his plate, and his hands shook. "The town would be better off if he dropped dead. He sits in that big house on the hill and lives the high life, while the rest of us scrape out a living in his factory."

"Marv, that's enough," Gloria said. "You lost your position because you were drinking on the job, and you know it."

"I did my work, and that bastard fired me. Came down from on high to do it himself, with this smug, satisfied look on his face."

"Are you still drinking?" Beau asked gently.

"What's it to you?" Marv snapped. From the smell and look of him, he clearly was, but making the judgment wasn't going to help.

Beau reached in his pocket, pulled out a card, and handed it to him. "If you want some help, come by." He had already learned that people had to want help if there was going to be any chance of success. He turned back to his lunch and ate slowly, checking the time. He was supposed to have dinner with Dante, and more and more, the picture of the man kept getting muddled.

What the hell had he gotten himself into?

CHAPTER 3

IT WAS Saturday and Dante still had work to do. He sat in his office, reviewing production reports and sales figures, which were all encouraging… with the exception of their artisan line, which had stagnated somewhat. A knock pulled him out of the reports, and Roberts came in with a tray.

"Where did you want to have dinner this evening?" Roberts set the tray on the corner of the desk and waited for an answer.

"He's coming to discuss business." Dante looked around the office and back to Roberts just in time to see him roll his eyes. "What is it?"

Roberts cleared his throat, his way of saying that Dante was being stupid without actually saying a word. "Mr. Beau is coming here for dinner at your invitation. I believe the proper thing to do is to prepare the dining room."

Dante raised his gaze. "It's business."

"I don't think so. It's a Saturday night. Normal people go out and have some fun because they don't go to work on Sunday. So my guess is that the business is a ruse." He met Dante's gaze for a second and then turned away, heading toward the door. "Shall I call to give you time to get ready?"

Dante picked up the papers, already engrossing his mind in them. "That would be great." He heard Roberts leave and picked up the cup of tea, then set it back down without drinking. Dante jumped up and left the office a few minutes later, following the sounds of activity through the living room and into the dining room, where the dust sheets had been pulled off all the furniture. Roberts carried them past him, while his housekeeper, Clare, cleaned the room like some sort of tornado. She paused in her work when she saw him, nodded, and continued.

"Roberts?" Dante called. "What's all this?"

Roberts kept his face neutral as he walked back into the room. "I told you the dining room would be appropriate and you didn't disagree, so we went ahead. I'm also removing the dust sheets in the living room and library. It's supposed to be cool this evening, so I'll have a fire built and serve brandy in there after dinner."

"Isn't this a little much?"

"No." Roberts walked away, leaving him standing near the head of the long walnut table.

Dante followed him into the other room, where Roberts was removing the dustcovers. "Roberts...." He let a growl slip into his voice. None of these rooms had been used since Allison died, and he wasn't sure if he was ready to open them up again.

"We can't entertain guests in a few rooms with the rest of the house closed up and unused." Roberts finished removing the covers and turned to survey the space. Dante did the same as a huge wave of regret washed over him. He had made so many mistakes when it came to Allison, and he hadn't been able to bear them, so he'd shut up most of the house and lived in the rooms that he could stand.

"Roberts, I never want to use these again."

"And you expect that nice Mr. Beau to eat Harriet's amazing dinner cooped up in your office?" He shook his head. "All right. I'll have everything put back the way it was."

"No." Dante turned, went back to his office, and closed the door. He needed a chance to breathe.

Allison had loved to entertain, and she'd used those rooms of the house all the time. They were the ones he most closely associated with her energy and vitality. At least those were the qualities she'd had when they'd been friends and had first gotten married. Before everything changed and Dante managed to mess up both their lives.

It had been over two years, and maybe it was time. If it had been up to him, those parts of the house would never have been opened up. But now they were, and apparently he and Beau were using them for their dinner and discussion. Roberts seemed to think this was something more than business. Did Beau think this was a date of some kind? Dante sat back at his desk, intending to return to work, but his mind had other ideas and he wasn't able to concentrate on anything.

"Sir, he'll be here in an hour. I laid out some clothes for you on your bed," Roberts said. Dante hadn't even heard him knock. "Harriet has made your favorite, beef Wellington. Unless you object, we'll serve appetizers in the sitting room." He held the door and stood silently, waiting for Dante.

"Roberts," Dante said as they began climbing the stairs a few minutes later. "When did you get so pushy?"

"Sir, I am the perfect servant. I know what you want before you do. It's my job. So I became 'pushy,' as you call it, when I realized it was what you needed." He opened the door to Dante's room and waited as he went inside.

"Thank you." Dante turned away and went into the bathroom, hearing Roberts leave. He wasn't sure if he should have been insulted at Roberts's answer or not. He wasn't, which surprised him. Dante also couldn't deny it. Since Allison's death he'd largely retreated from his own life, and other than business, he lived in a very small circle. He had everything he thought he wanted, but maybe he hadn't understood what that was.

Dante started the shower and undressed, ignoring the mirror the entire time. He hated looking in them, always afraid of what he was going to see looking back at him.

He knew what people called him. He'd heard the comments; it was hard not to, now that he knew what to listen for. But what also ate at his heart was that he knew they were right. Dante had been beastly in the past, and that had cost him the close friend who'd agreed to become his wife. He'd made a bargain with the devil himself, in the form of his own bloody father, and that had cost himself everything—including a part of his soul that he would never be able to retrieve. So sometimes he wondered if the beast he felt inside him, the one who had sold his own and his best friend's futures out from under them, would glare at him from the glass.

He stepped under the water and pulled the shower door closed. He used the tea tree oil soap from the dish, luxuriating in the lather and mild scent. It soothed him, but he had no idea why. Closing his eyes, he was shocked when it brought up images of Beau. His slightly crooked nose and full lips, the small turn to his eyeteeth—all of it fell to the background when his stunningly deep blue eyes forced their way forward, making Dante wonder what they hid. The water was hot, but Dante shivered for a second at what those eyes might have seen and comprehended.

No one asked him anything unless they wanted something from him. He wasn't invited to dinner to discuss deals. People made appointments, came, and then left as quickly as their legs and cars could carry them. Beau had asked him to dinner, and for the thousandth time, Dante wondered what it meant.

Without realizing it, he'd slipped back out of the water and had soaped his chest and belly, his hands dipping lower until his fingers wrapped around and slid along his now-throbbing length. As long as he kept his eyes closed, he saw Beau looking back at him, eyes intensely watching his, lips curling upward, parting slightly. Dante wondered what they tasted like, what they'd feel like against his, on his skin, around him, sliding deeper. But it was what they'd be like when Dante took possession of them, sliding his tongue between them, taking Beau in hand, watching his eyes as they turned the color of the deepest water, and the tiniest hint of the word *please* on his lips, that sent Dante over the edge.

Breathing deeply, he placed one hand on the tile wall to steady himself, water cascading over him, washing away the soap and everything else. Finally, once he could move again, Dante turned off the water and stepped out of the shower. He used the luxurious towels to dry his still-tingling skin before entering his bedroom and starting to dress.

The pants Roberts had laid out were dark gray but soft, and the shirt—silk that shimmered over his chest, caressing it like a lover—made him close his eyes once again. He hadn't been touched in that way in so very long. Dante didn't deserve it and never would again. He pulled on his socks, woven from bamboo fibers, and then slipped on his shoes.

Roberts knocked and came inside to look him over. "Yes. That will do very nicely."

"This is a business meeting," Dante groaned, but Roberts merely cleared his throat and waited. It was so annoying. "Yes?"

"I never thought you were that obtuse." Roberts left the room, pulling the door closed, and Dante growled into the empty space. If Roberts was going to be matchmaking, Dante was going to have to put him in his place, fast.

He strode to the door, pulled it open with more force than was necessary, and barreled out into the hall toward the stairs. He took them at damn near a run, building up a head of steam, then came to a halt in the entrance hall when he saw Roberts taking Beau's jacket.

Dante had seen him in that god-awful, ill-fitting tuxedo, as well as those terrible clothes he wore at the Center that looked like they'd been chosen by a blind man feeling his way through a jumbled-up secondhand clothing store. But the plain, light blue button-down that hugged his upper arms just a touch and the light charcoal pants that hugged his hips and accentuated his narrow waist displayed just what Beau had been hiding. He might not have been handsome in the classic way, but he was eye-catching, and when Dante's gaze reached his eyes, the energy in them, like waves on the water, took his breath away.

"Thank you for coming," Dante said, extending his arm toward the living room.

Beau clutched a bottle of wine in his hands as though it were a life preserver. "Thank you for having me." He handed Dante the bottle, and Roberts stepped forward, but Dante shook his head once and carried it with him into the living room. "I wasn't sure what to bring to…." Beau quieted as he looked around the room. "Holy cow." He lifted his gaze, mouth hanging open. "I've seen things like this in books but never in person."

"My great-grandfather started the porcelain works, and he built the house as a twenty-fifth anniversary gift for his wife. Well, actually, he let her build it. Apparently my great-grandmother had a love for architecture, and she designed the house. I'm told this room was one of her favorites. She adored rich woods and used them throughout this floor." The focal point of the room was a grand fireplace, surrounded in hand-painted tiles specifically designed for the house and executed at the works. The surround included a wide mantel that went all the way to the ceiling. Next to it were two pedestals in marble with large bronzes of Greek gods. The walnut display cases on the far end of the room held examples of the decorative porcelains they'd produced over the decades, including some of the earliest and rarest pieces that collectors would kill for now. In short, this room was designed to impress.

Dante set the wine on the coffee table and motioned Beau to one of the large, overstuffed club chairs. His great-grandmother had them custom-made for this room, and they had been reupholstered over the years. And as Dante sat down, he remembered how much he loved them.

"I appreciate you having me over." Beau sat stiffly, his back straight and hands clenched. "I have some ideas for some new programs…. We offer counseling and treatment at the Center, working with two local doctors, but I'd really like to be able to have a doctor—a psychiatrist—on staff. The programs we have are ones to support people's treatment and recovery. I'd like to be able to offer access to quality primary mental health to people who can't afford it."

Dante raised an eyebrow. "That's very ambitious."

"Yes, and it would take the support required to hire a staff doctor, which is expensive. I'd like to look to Baltimore or

Washington to recruit someone, along with a psychiatric nurse and even a medical practitioner to act as support. I have a feeling that once these services become available, they will be in great demand." Beau cleared his throat. "I want to say that I'm not asking you to write a check for this. A free ride isn't what I'm talking about. You're the town's most prominent citizen, though, so your support would be invaluable."

Dante cleared his throat, trying to remove the lump that wouldn't go away. He couldn't say how much it pleased him that Beau wasn't simply asking him to write a check, like so many others thought he should. "I don't know what the town would think about that." As soon as he'd said it, he wished he'd kept his thought to himself. "The Foundation could certainly provide you with help. We have people who could work with you to write grant applications, and we could pledge some startup funds that would boost your applications."

"That would be great. I believe in the 'teach a man to fish' philosophy."

"I wish others did." Dante looked up as Roberts came in with a tray and set it on the table.

"Would you like me to chill the wine?" Roberts asked, and Dante nodded, his attention on Beau. Roberts left the room, and Dante lifted the plate of bruschetta, sprinkled with a touch of Parmesan, offering one to Beau.

"Is that what you wanted to talk to me about?" Dante asked. He got the idea there was more to it. Beau's eyes were a dead giveaway, telling him so much. "I suppose you're wondering about me. Everyone does."

The mirth that filled Beau's eyes was priceless and something Dante hadn't seen in anyone in a long time. "Full of yourself much?" Beau teased, and Dante tried to remember the last time anyone had done that… and failed. Beau took a bite, humming under his breath. He took the second bite and used one of the napkins to wipe his fingers, watching him, stripping Dante naked under that intense gaze. Beau must see something in him others didn't, and it scared the shit out of him. He didn't ask anything, just continued to watch, and Dante squirmed in his chair. It was so unnerving, and he hadn't acted that way since that fatefully awful conversation with his father.

"Where did you move from?" Dante asked, figuring it was better to get the focus off him.

"Silver Spring. My stepmom and dad live there. He works for the Interior Department, and my mom is an economist for the Congressional Budget Office. They're pretty cool, given all they've been through. I have an older sister who is a doctor in Bethesda."

"Is she who you had in mind with this new position?"

"Good God, no. She's an orthopedist. And I love my family, but they tend to get too much into my life. So if my sister decided to move here, I'd probably need my own counseling services because I'd develop a drinking problem." Beau chuckled. "Don't get me wrong, I love her, but in smaller doses. She's a big sister and thinks she has to look out for me... for that matter, so do my mom and dad."

There was a story there; Dante could feel Beau skirting around it. He didn't want to ask what it was because he had plenty of stories himself that he had every intention of taking to his grave.

"Do you have any siblings?" Beau asked.

"No. My parents only had me. Dad worked a lot, and my mom... let's just say she could have used your services. I think she was lonely a lot of the time, and she decided to ease some of that with a bottle. She was a sneaky drinker, hiding it and slipping away to get what she wanted. I was fourteen when her system gave out. I wasn't told what happened in any detail, and I nearly had to browbeat my father into telling me, but he finally did." Dante shook his head. "I know this probably isn't the best time, but would you like something to drink?"

"The white wine I brought would be nice." Beau seemed nervous and once again looked around the room. "I don't drink a great deal, but I like a glass of wine every once in a while."

"Of course."

Roberts's timing was impeccable, and he entered with glasses and two bottles, which he placed on the side table.

"White for both of us," Dante said.

"Does he always do that?" Beau asked in a whisper, glancing at Roberts, who brought over the glasses of wine, handing one to each of them.

"Dinner will be in an hour," Roberts said softly and then left the room.

"Is he going to come back again?"

Dante shook his head. "He's done for a while. Sometimes I swear he has ESP or something." He sipped the wine. "Would you like to see the rest of the house?"

Beau's eyes lit up. "Yes."

Dante stood and waited for Beau. "This is the public portion of the house. The other side of the hall has my private office, then a family room, the breakfast room, and solarium at the back. My mother used to keep that room full of tropical plants, but now it's largely empty." He motioned to the door at the back of the room. "This is the library. When the house was built, this was the men's domain after dinner—the ladies would use the living room—then after cigars and brandy, maybe some business, they'd rejoin the ladies."

Beau went into the room, lined with bookshelves on three walls, all behind glass doors. "Are all these…?" His voice faded to a whisper as though he were in church.

"Yes. All four generations of Bartholomew men collected books. My great-grandfather bought a library from England and had the books shipped over here. There are illuminated manuscripts and an early Shakespeare volume. The three empty cases are ones we have yet to fill." He let Beau wander the room while he sipped his wine and wondered why he'd gone this long and let this much of his history and past be shut away. He knew the answer, but he never should have let it go on for so long.

"What's over there?" Beau asked, pointing to the other door when they stepped out.

"The dining room." The space glittered with crystal and gold doré centerpieces. The light was low and glowed off the chandelier, shining on the table surface, warming the already rich, polished wood. Roberts had clearly gone all out to impress tonight. "Through there is the kitchen, but Harriet will not be pleased if we get underfoot."

"Holy cow. This is beautiful." Beau ran his fingers lightly over the table surface. "This is a beautiful home."

"There's more. Great-grandmother really liked to entertain. She apparently believed that in order to get ahead in business, you needed to wine and dine." Dante unlatched one of the wood panels and pulled the hidden door open, then swung the second panel into the room.

"What's this?" Beau slowly moved into the large space.

"The ballroom." Sheets covered the chandeliers, like fat ghosts hanging upside down from the ceiling. The furniture along the walls was also covered, and a layer of dust lay on the floor. The walls were frescoes of garden scenes that would shimmer under the lights at night between floor-to-ceiling windows. "As you can see, this hasn't been used in quite a long time."

"I bet she had live music over there, with tables for food and a dance floor." Beau wandered through the room.

"There's more than that." Dante opened the grand doors at the end of the room. "When she had larger parties, she'd have them in here. This table is in three sections, with leaves that will connect to one another to a length of twenty-four feet. My mother never entertained that many people, so basically this has been the least used room in the house recently. My dad had a sound system installed with the intention of having conferences for the business here. That didn't work out either."

Dante's footsteps echoed in the empty room as he walked back toward the dining room door. He waited for Beau and closed the room off once more, then headed back to the living room. They had a few more appetizers and enjoyed their wine, talking a little until Roberts called them in for dinner.

Dante stood near his seat, waiting for Beau to sit before he took his own. Roberts served each of them and then left the room once again.

"Is there something going on with him? He keeps looking at me funny." Beau seemed slightly nervous.

Dante shook his head. "Roberts has this idea that this is some sort of date." He smiled as though to laugh the idea off, but Beau stared seriously at him. Dante groaned softly, seeing what everyone else had already caught on to.

"I didn't mean this as a *date*-date I guess. But I didn't ask you to dinner just to pitch you my idea." Beau cut a bite of his Wellington, eyes downcast.

"Then why?" It wasn't as though people were beating a path to the Beast of St. Giles's door to ask him dancing, not in this town. When he was away and no one knew the reputation he had in town, things were different, at least somewhat. It wasn't like Dante was a party-type guy. Most of his travel was for business, which he took very seriously.

Beau shrugged. "I don't understand you," he finally answered, then took a bite. "You have this reputation in the town, and everyone talks about you all the time. The things they say are as cruel and judgmental as I've ever heard. They made up a name for you."

"Yes… I know." Dante narrowed his eyes, trying to keep his temper in check.

"I saw you rip the mayor to shreds and heard you on the phone when you were in the Center. You weren't very nice. But then, with Bobby at the dinner and the kids at the Center, you were patient and kind, even going out of your way to be caring. So what's the real you?"

Dante sighed. "All of them—both. I like kids. They aren't demanding and they don't have agendas. What you see is what you get. Secrets never stay that way for very long with them. They don't generally hide who they are, and they don't look at me as though I'm the devil himself." He wasn't sure how much to say, but he didn't want Beau to have any illusions either. "When I'm with kids, I can forget what I've done and just be myself, the person I want to be." He set down his fork.

"Are you saying the rumors are right?" Beau was clearly shocked, judging by the way his eyes widened and his sharp intake of breath.

"I suppose in every rumor, there's a nugget of truth at the core of it." Dante waved his hand because he wasn't going to dissect each and every one of the stories. "There are things that I've done in my life, decisions I made that I have to pay for."

"But you were married?" Beau asked. "Maybe I'm dumb, but I thought, with the way you were looking at me, that you're gay... the way I am." He lowered his gaze to the table but not before his cheeks turned cherry red.

"I was married, and...." Dante's thoughts turned to Allison and his throat constricted. He reached for his water and took a sip. "I made some decisions that caused people close to me a great deal of pain." Suddenly his defenses rose. "I have to live with that and pay for it. As for any details, I will not talk about it. Those decisions led to my wife's death." He picked up his knife and fork and returned to his dinner, needing something to do. He could feel Beau's gaze on him like a blowtorch. He'd invited Beau to the house because he hadn't wanted to go out in town and have people talking about him. He'd thought this would be a safe environment, except at the moment he felt uncomfortable in his own house.

Dante ate without talking, the dishes and glasses tinkling occasionally.

"Maybe this wasn't such a good idea." Beau set his silverware on his plate with a sour note. "Everyone has secrets and things that they aren't proud of. You say that kids don't have any hidden agendas. But maybe you can't be happy until you start to give up your own hidden agenda and try to live your life honestly." He pushed his chair back and stood. "Thank you for the tour and for dinner. I appreciate the invitation and the talk, but I think it's best—"

Dante stood as well. "It's been a long time since I entertained anyone, and if I was rude, I apologize." He waited until Beau slowly sat back down. "It's also been a long time since I talked about myself, and as you can tell, I'm not my favorite subject." He'd been abrupt, and clearly his social skills needed some improvement. "Is the food all right?" When in doubt, change the subject… at almost all costs.

"It's delicious." Beau took another bite and sipped his wine. "I know you don't want to talk about it, but maybe you should. I'm not necessarily saying you should with me, though I'd be willing to listen, but you definitely should with someone. Secrets and pain have a way of growing and becoming bigger over time unless we deal with them."

"Is that the counselor talking?" Dante finished his beef and cut his green beans into smaller pieces, eating them slowly.

"No. I'm saying that as a friend."

Dante didn't know what to think of that. He hadn't had a friend in a long time. After getting married and with the relationship falling apart, most of his friends had drifted away for one reason or another. Then after Allison died and the rumors began, those few who had stuck by him up till then had basically run for the hills. Not that he'd done anything to keep them. "Then I'll think about it." Dante knew there was little to think about. Nothing could change the past. It was written in stone. "Would you like some more?" He stood and brought the dishes over from the server, then returned to his seat. "Harriet will be disappointed if we don't make a dent in this."

"How long has she worked here?"

"My mother found her ten years ago when she was working at a restaurant in St. Michaels. Mom used to go in once a week, and she was impressed enough to offer her the job here. Harriet and Allison didn't get along, and she nearly quit." He didn't go into the fact that she only stayed because Allison was no longer in the picture. "After dinner, I'll brave the kitchen and introduce you. She's a very nice lady. She just guards her kitchen as her private domain and has everything in its place."

"It seems like everyone here...." Beau stumbled. "They're different and they seem to care about you."

"I like to think so."

"See. That's another thing that's perplexing. If you were as bad a person as the rumors say or as you think you are, then why does your staff act like they do?" Beau raised his eyebrows. "Do you want to know what I think?"

Dante honestly wasn't sure, but he nodded anyway.

"I think there's a lot more to you than meets the eye, and...." He paused. "I think you get along with your staff because you're basically a good person."

Dante rolled his eyes and nearly snorted. "I get along with my staff because I treat them well, reward them, and let them do their jobs. There isn't a whole lot more to it than that." He wasn't going to allow this particular line of inquiry and intended to cut it off. He was who he was and didn't like people analyzing him. He had his motives for behaving the way he did and they were his own. Period. He set his jaw and was seconds from folding his arms over his chest to signal this particular conversation was over. But Beau either didn't notice or didn't care, because he seemed intent on plowing forward.

"I also think you get along with those kids because you have a lot in common with them." Beau's voice grew softer and gentle, and Dante's spine relaxed back in the chair. "I assume that you had more than one person in your life who was a substance abuser." Beau swallowed and gazed at him with sympathy and understanding rather than an accusation or pity, the way he would have expected.

Dante was at a complete loss how to respond. Thankfully he didn't have to. Roberts entered and efficiently cleared the dishes, then returned with coffee and two plates of dessert before leaving them alone once again. The apple tartlets smelled as cinnamon-sweet as Dante could have imagined. He inhaled and closed his eyes, letting the scent bring back happier memories. "My mother used to make apple pies," he said softly.

"Scent memories are very strong," Beau agreed and also inhaled. "This reminds me of the fall, when my mother would drive us to the orchards and she and I would pick apples. She was into locally grown food decades before other people. We used to pick berries, peaches, cherries, apples, pears—all of it." Beau smiled. "Never pick cherries. Worst thing on earth. After a while, they're juicy enough and it runs down your hands and arms." He may have been complaining, but there was an upturn to his lips.

"Sir…." Roberts bustled into the room again, which was highly unusual behavior. He had one efficient pace and stuck to it. "There are people out by the front drive, and they have signs."

Dante set down his fork. "Excuse me."

"I think they're picketers of some sort." Roberts stepped back, giving him room. Dante stood, placing his napkin on the table, and turned to stride into the hall. He pulled open the front door and stepped out into the night. He didn't hear anything, but flashes of white near the drive entrance caught his eye. He walked down the driveway toward the small group of people on the sidewalk, who did indeed have signs, proclaiming: "Bartholomew Unfair Employment Practices," "Wrongful Termination," and "Sink the Beast." Dante barely paused before strolling to the first woman he recognized.

"We're on public property," she said quickly… too quickly.

"That may be, but I know you and I know your husband," he said loudly enough for all of them to hear as he stopped, pulling himself to his full height, hands on his hips. "I suggest you all go home before other employment needs are evaluated." He met the gaze of each person. "Now!" The snap in his voice echoed off the house and rolled back to him, like a roar into the night. If they were going to call him a beast, he'd sure as hell act like it.

They looked at one another, doubt creeping in. "This is peaceful, and we're entitled to our opinion," another of the women said, the wife of another of his employees.

"True, but I am entitled to employ who I wish and you know it." He met her eyes with a glare he knew would test her resolve.

"And you'd better get your facts straight before you come at me in the night with your signs. Now go!" He pointed down the road, glaring at each of them in turn. Dante didn't turn away as their resolve crumbled before his eyes. Without waiting around any longer, he strode back to the house and went inside, pushing the door closed with a thud that rang through the hall. Then he turned back toward the dining room and nearly ran into Beau, who was as white as a sheet.

"What was that about?" Beau asked in the same gentle tone he'd used earlier.

Dante ground his teeth. "Misled busybodies who don't have a clue about anything deciding they're going to stick their noses where they don't belong." He sat at the table and waited for Beau. "I'm the head of Bartholomew Porcelain, and I'm the one who makes the decisions. Good or bad, I do what's best for the company." He snatched up his fork and turned, waiting for Beau, who came in more slowly and stood next to his chair. "Right or wrong I take responsibility for my actions. It's part of running the company so it will be around in a year, a decade, and maybe longer."

"I don't understand all this," Beau said, still pale.

"What's there to understand? They weren't happy with my decision and thought they could bully me into getting something that's impossible… and ridiculous. Besides, it's not my life's goal to make them happy." Dante dropped his fork to the table. "I don't owe them anything. Not one single solitary thing. I keep the factory running, do good work for the town, give back all the time… and I'm vilified. Well, they can take a flying leap, and I do intend to speak to the supervisors on Monday, make sure they know that this sort of thing will not be tolerated." His heart rate finally began returning to normal, and by the time he picked up his fork once more, he realized Beau wasn't in the room just before he heard the front door close.

CHAPTER 4

BEAU HAD been second-guessing himself for three days. He'd always been taught not to be rude, but he had truly gotten a glimpse... or at least heard one... of the Beast that night. There had been no care or consideration in his voice whatsoever.

"Honey, I tried to warn you." Angie patted his hand lightly.

Beau was grateful for her sincerity, since it must have taken extra effort for her not to do some sort of I-told-you-so dance. "I know you did." He just couldn't seem to put things together in his mind.

"Then what's wrong?" Angie pressed.

The truth was, he couldn't get Dante out of his head. He kept seeing him as he showed him through the largely empty house, gentle, smiling, even laughing occasionally. "I was so rude...." Beau had also blown any chance he had for securing Dante's help to expand the services the Center could offer—completely blown it.

"You just left. That's so unlike you." Angie leaned forward, and Beau followed her gaze toward a noise in the hallway.

"I know. I kind of freaked out a little. The way he talked to those people by the front of his house was so harsh, and.... All I kept thinking was that I was seeing the Beast that everyone keeps talking about, and it was not pretty at all."

"Just stay away from the guy and have as little to do with him as possible. We're all better off if we can survive without him or his money. People in this town have come to rely on it too much, and now they complain about him, but they can't do a dang thing about it. They need him."

Beau nodded slowly. "But he needs everyone else too, and I don't think he knows it."

Angie shook her head. "You know what's going on here? You're too damn nice. You see him as one of the people here that you can help, but you can't. You know that, because he doesn't want to be helped. You always say that we can't do anything with someone who doesn't want our help, and the Beast definitely doesn't think there's anything wrong with him."

The fire of righteous condemnation burned brightly in her eyes, but Beau knew she wasn't completely right. Dante had admitted to him that night at dinner that there was something wrong. He was carrying around a mountain full of guilt over something, and Beau suspected it was his wife's death. But Dante wasn't going to talk about it, and there was no one to ask about what had happened. So Angie was correct—there was nothing Beau could do to help unless Dante came to trust him enough to confide in Beau with what happened. But after the way Beau left the other night, he'd blown that chance out of the water.

"Why is this bothering you so much?" Angie asked, raising her eyebrows slightly. "You don't have some sort of crush on him, do you?"

"I don't think so." Beau wasn't sure what his feelings were toward Dante Bartholomew. He intrigued him and he was certainly good-looking enough... in every way Beau had seen.

Angie humphed. "That's an interesting answer. Do you want to explain?"

Beau smiled wickedly. "No, I don't." Dammit, he was blushing and he hated that. He couldn't seem to get Dante out of his head, even after Dante's behavior had left him cold. "I'm confused, okay? And I hate being all mixed up." Beau smiled. "When we were having dinner, there was this moment when he forgot himself. I don't even think he realized it at the time, but the tiny lines around his eyes disappeared and his lips were soft and there was this light in his eyes. Dante laughed, and in that second, I thought I might be seeing the real person under the hurt, pain, responsibility, and God knows what else he's carrying around, and I want to see more of that person. Then I saw him with those protestors, throwing his weight around and—"

"You thought you'd imagined everything, and the real person was the Beast throwing his weight around?"

Man, she could hit the nail on the head.

"I don't want him to be that person." Beau turned and walked away from Angie's desk. He had a pile of work waiting for him on his desk, and it wasn't going to do him any good to vacillate over Dante. He'd really blown that opportunity.

HE SPENT the next two hours knee-deep in his paperwork, trying to catch up. Beau tended to let it pile up because he hated it and would rather spend time with the people who came to him for help. That was what he loved. But he needed to do the paperwork that would allow him to do what he enjoyed.

"Beau," Angie said, half breathless. "The Beast is out front asking for you. He says he wants to talk to you." She cocked her lips in a slightly off-kilter way. "He's carrying flowers." She snickered and rolled her eyes. "Is that just too cheesy for words?"

Beau sighed. "Not everyone wants their men to say they care with a visit to the gun club." He winked, and Angie crossed her arms over her chest.

"I knew I was going to regret telling you about that date."

Beau stood. "Hey, you had a good time, and that's all that counts. And the fact that you outshot him was completely priceless." He glanced down at the work he had yet to finish and groaned softly. "Tell Dante I'll be out in a few minutes." He sat back down to finish reviewing a grant application before giving it his approval and then went to see what Dante wanted from him.

Angie sat at her desk, typing and watching Dante at the same time. It was weird how she could work and watch him at the same time… until Beau peered at her screen and saw the gibberish she was typing. He kept her secret as he walked by.

"Can I help you, Dante?" Beau was proud of himself for keeping things professional and his eyes on Dante's instead of raking them down to his tight jeans.

"Is there somewhere we can talk? Privately."

"My office is right down the hall." He motioned, and Dante followed him inside the tiny space. It was utilitarian and nothing like the office Dante had at his house. Beau closed the door and sat in the second visitor's chair, waiting for Dante, who seemed to be searching for his words.

"I never explain anything to anyone," Dante pronounced as he handed Beau the flowers. "Explanations are too close to excuses, and my father drilled into me that excuses were unacceptable and apologizing is a sign of weakness."

"You know that's bullshit... right?" Beau smelled the flowers and stifled the sneeze that threatened. He loved flowers, but some of them didn't love him back.

"Does it matter? My father pounded that in deeper than the pilings for the Bay Bridge. He never said he was sorry for anything, not even to my mother, and he never stood for any sort of excuses, only logical arguments." Dante huffed. "Anyway, I don't do explanations, but I think you deserve one." He shifted in his seat the way a kid might when he was called to the principal's office.

"Why?" Beau questioned. "If you don't do them, then why tell me?"

Dante leaned closer. "I don't fucking know why. But... I think for some stupid reason, I care what you think about me."

Beau nodded slowly and thought he might have been given a glimpse, even as small as it was, into how Dante thought about things. "You really don't care what other people think?"

Dante shrugged. "Being a leader means thinking for yourself. Yeah, you listen to others, but you have to be the one making the decisions, and sometimes they're hard. So, no, I don't usually care what people think of me. But I care how you see me." Dante looked nervous and worked up, fidgeting in his seat.

"What do you want to tell me?"

"When I was here working with the kids, I got a phone call. One of the men at the plant, in the accounting department, we caught him stealing from the company."

"Is that why you were so angry?" Beau remembered that call and how Dante had sounded. "You were cold as hell."

Dante nodded. "The porcelain works has been doing well and sales keep improving, but our profits have flatlined over the last two years and I couldn't figure it out. Then I got the call that day that John Lederer, the plant head, had stumbled onto something and found the cause. I had the man's employment terminated. Apparently he told his wife that I let him go for no reason because, after all, I'm the Beast of St. Giles and everything that happens here is somehow my fault."

"So they showed up at your house with picket signs…."

"Yeah. They wanted to try to pressure me to give Greg his job back, but that isn't going to happen. We've tracked down some of the money he stole, but most of it is gone forever. I know what I said to them and how I treated those people, but they had no clue what was going on and they came to my home to send me a message." Dante paused briefly. "I work hard to carry the family business forward, which keeps the town prosperous and employs most of the families here in one way or another. I could keep all the money and make myself rich, but I send most of the profits to the Foundation, where it's given back to the community."

"Is that all you do?" Beau asked.

"No. I protect the people in my life. I don't have many of them, but I guard the people who work for me, and I will not tolerate anyone intruding on what should be my private life. They brought some imagined fight to my doorstep and expected me to roll over and take it. I won't."

"I think I can understand that. But you get more flies with honey than you do with vinegar."

"Maybe, but people fuck with you less if you let them know that you aren't going to take it."

The near-raging fire behind Dante's eyes was really telling and helped convince Beau that he had been right: Dante's life had been incredibly unpredictable and abusive. But Beau wasn't going to press it right now. Dante wasn't going to tell him what was behind all of this. He'd kept it bottled up inside for a very long time, and never letting go was too wrapped up in who Dante had become.

"Was that all you wanted to tell me?" Beau asked, sitting back in the chair. He was used to waiting people out, though Dante seemed like a tough nut. He crossed his legs and got a little more comfortable.

"I had a good time at dinner… well, before…."

"I understand." Beau was getting an idea where this conversation was headed, but he purposely let Dante stumble a little in order to let him decide what he really wanted. Many of the people he worked with had trouble making decisions because they didn't understand what it was they truly wanted. Others had decisions made for them their whole lives, and part of Beau's job was to empower them so they felt as though they could make decisions for themselves.

"Would you like to try to have dinner again?" Dante finally asked.

Beau nodded. "Yes. That would be very nice. But this time, let's go out to dinner. There's a nice restaurant in St. Michaels."

"I was thinking that Harriet could make dinner for us again and—"

"No. You asked me properly, and I'd like to go out like a real person. Give your staff the night off, and we can have some fun." Beau pulled up his calendar. "I don't have any appointments tomorrow evening or on Friday or Saturday. We could go then if you'd like." Beau waited. "I understand why you don't venture into town here a lot. But I think you're making a mistake."

Dante leaned forward. "Excuse me?"

Beau thought a second. "Unless you *want* people to think of you as the Beast?" He was trying to get a reaction from Dante, and instead Dante leaned back and ignored that part of the comment.

"How am I making a mistake… in your opinion?" Dante was humoring him, which was so clear from the amusement in his tone.

"People talk about and make up stories about people they don't know. Ethnic jokes are made about other groups of people. If you went out and met people, let them see you and maybe talk to you, they'd realize you aren't a monster."

Dante closed his eyes. "But what if I am?" He stood, went to the door, and pulled it open. Then he stepped out into the hall, and Beau figured he'd pushed too hard and was already swearing silently at himself in his head.

Beau lowered his gaze and was about to get up so he could put the flowers in water.

"Tomorrow night would be nice," Dante said. "Let me know where you'd like me to pick you up." He closed the door, leaving Beau in shock.

He sat still for a few seconds, then snatched up the phone. "Angie, come in here a second."

The door opened almost before he hung up the phone. "He gave you the flowers?" she asked as Beau handed them to her.

"Put them in some water and set them on the front desk so everyone can enjoy them." His eyes were already starting to water. He tried to stop it, but his sneeze rang through the small room.

"You didn't tell him you were allergic, did you?" She took them and stepped out of the office as Beau sneezed again.

"Of course not. It was a nice gesture, and no one has ever given me flowers." He wiped his eyes and turned back to his desk.

She leaned down, inhaling the scent of the yellow and orange roses. "Was that all?"

Beau wagged his eyebrows and said nothing more.

"No way? The Beast asked you out?" Her lower lip nearly hit the floor.

"Angie, we don't talk about people, anyone, like that here. Please don't anymore. Okay? This is a safe place, and that means from bullying of any kind." He shot her a brief but stern look before

64

checking the clock. He had a few minutes for some paperwork before he had a group session.

AFTER WORK the next day, Beau walked home and climbed the stairs. He liked the place. It wasn't too old, and the appliances were relatively new. He didn't have a lot of furniture; what he'd gotten had come from a few secondhand stores. Nothing matched, but he didn't mind. It was his and the furniture was comfortable. He loved his sofa in particular. It was extra wide, and on cold evenings, he curled up on it under a blanket and watched television as he fell asleep.

Beau checked the time and hurried to the bathroom. He had fifteen minutes to clean up and dress. He showered fast and pulled on a pair of dark gray dress pants and a pale green shirt. He checked himself in the mirror, grabbed his shoes and socks, then looked out the window for Dante before pulling them on. Then he checked again, locked up, and went down the stairs to the sidewalk. Beau checked his phone for the time and glanced up as a long black limousine pulled to a stop. The back door opened, and Dante smiled out at him.

"I don't think this was necessary," Beau said as he got inside and closed the door, and the vehicle glided away from the curb. "Do you have a driver too?"

"In a way. Roberts runs the inside of the house, and Juan manages the exterior. He also acts as my driver on occasion."

"Doesn't that make for long days?"

"Sometimes. But when his son graduated from high school, he used the limousine, and again when his daughter got married. I don't go everywhere in it, so I don't need a full-time driver, but I thought it would make tonight special." Dante sat back as they rode out of town and to the main road that led south down toward St. Michaels. "Is seafood okay?"

"Of course," Beau answered as he tried to relax. "It's what the town is known for."

"I made a reservation, but I haven't been there in a few years. Thankfully Roberts had a suggestion. I hope it's okay."

Dante was acting nervous, and that made Beau rather happy in a perverse way. He reached forward, turning up the air-conditioning a little so he didn't sweat through his shirt. Okay, so maybe he was nervous too.

"I wasn't expecting to see you... today... or ever again. Not after how I left."

"I was pretty upset when you disappeared. But then, I guess I brought it on myself." Dante's leg bounced slightly, and Beau let his gaze travel from his mirror-shiny shoes up his black-clad leg to where the fabric gripped Dante's thighs. Beau's mouth turned dry in an instant. "I've brought on a lot of my own grief over the years."

Beau could have easily slipped into counselor mode, but that wasn't his role tonight. Instead, he put on a different hat, so to speak, took Dante's hand, and threaded their fingers together. "Maybe it's time for you to stop adding to the pile of whatever it is you see as your grief."

Dante turned to look at him. "Spoken like a true counselor."

"Is that what you think I'm here to do? Is that why you invited me to dinner? Did you want some one-on-one counseling time?" Beau tightened his fingers. "Because that isn't why I'm here, and all you had to do for that was call and make an appointment. It's free, in part because of your generosity."

"No. That's not why I asked you out." Dante huffed. "Sometimes you can be as prickly as anyone I've ever met."

Beau rolled his eyes. "That's the pot calling the kettle black, and you know it." He grinned, and Dante followed suit. "There...."

"What?"

"You smiled." Beau reached over and gently ran his fingers over Dante's cheek, then up into his raven-black hair, its softness lightly tickling his fingers. "You're stunning when you smile."

Dante closed his eyes and sighed softly without moving. "So are you."

"No, I'm not. I know I'm rather plain-looking and not all that special. I don't have your chiseled jawline or…." Beau pulled his hand away and rested it on his lap. "I'm not handsome and I never will be."

Dante leaned closer. "How about you let me decide what you are."

The hint of growl in his voice went right down Beau's spine, settled in his groin, and took root in the most energetic and erotic way. Beau shifted for comfort and wished he dared reposition himself. He stretched his leg out, grateful for the space provided.

"You don't understand," Beau said softly.

"About what?" Dante stroked Beau's cheek. "I think you're handsome and kind of cute." Dante smiled again. Beau was about to protest the cute remark, but Dante ran his thumb over his lower lip, and his protest died there.

Dante leaned forward, bringing their lips together, and Beau's brain short-circuited. The touch was light and gentle at first, but as Beau put his arms around Dante's neck, the kiss heated and Dante's weight against him increased, pressing him back.

The fire between them flared white-hot, and Beau tried to control it but lost. Dante cupped Beau's head in his hand and took possession of him. Beau capitulated in seconds, giving Dante whatever he asked for because it was exactly what Beau wanted as well. Dante tasted of mint and man mixed in heady proportions. It was all Beau could have asked for. He leaned back under Dante's weight and lay on the seat, looking up into Dante's passion-darkened eyes. Beau was blown away. Never in his life had anyone looked at him that way… with enough heat to melt steel. Speaking of steel, that's what pressed against the front of Beau's pants, desperate for release, and Beau felt an answering rod against his for a few seconds.

Dante pulled him closer, kissing harder. The leather of the seat cradled his body, the car rocking slightly as it traveled over the road. Not that Beau felt much of anything other than the pounding of his heart. He pulled back, taking in the intensity in Dante's eyes. He wanted Beau. There was no doubt of that, not for a second. Beau groaned under his breath at the warmth in Dante's gaze.

"You taste like passion," Dante told him in a whisper that rumbled through Beau's brain like a freight train. "I want more of you… I want—"

Beau closed his eyes and the distance between them. He had to cut off Dante's words, and that was the only way to do it fast enough. His mind grew so clouded, he barely registered Dante undoing the buttons of his shirt. But as soon as Dante's hand pressed to his chest, Beau grew still, clamping his eyes closed.

"What happened to you?" Dante asked as he pulled away.

Beau didn't dare open his eyes or he'd see the pity and disgust on Dante's face, and that was something he couldn't stand. Not after what he'd just felt.

"Beau…." Dante held his shirt, but Beau pulled away, doing up the buttons as quickly as he could.

"I know it isn't pretty." Beau opened his eyes and sat back up, cursing himself for ever letting any of this happen. He liked Dante and found him… so many things. Hell, he was attracted to him, but that attraction had blinded him to the facts he hid under his clothing each and every day. There was a reason he only ever opened the top button on his shirts and never wore V-neck T-shirts or tank tops.

"What happened to you?" Dante asked again.

"It doesn't matter. It was a long time ago, and there's nothing I can do about it." Beau crossed his arms over his chest to add some additional armor. The ardor of just a minute earlier had evaporated within seconds, and now they were just riding to dinner.

"It must have been painful."

Beau nodded. He always told his clients that holding things inside was never good and only allowed them to fester and grow.

Beau had come to terms with what had happened and how he looked a long time ago. At least he liked to tell himself that, but his reaction at Dante's touch said maybe that wasn't true. "They thought I was going to die." His belly did a few little flips and then settled down. "I don't remember it much. I was thirteen. My dad loved to hunt. It was his passion. He'd dreamed of hunting in the Upper Peninsula of Michigan, so he and I got licenses and we went up there for the opening of deer season." He remembered it like it was yesterday. "I used to love going out with him. The trees and the quiet were enticing. With all the leaves falling, it was one of the best times for me to go outside. I had really bad allergies as a kid. I've outgrown a lot of them now."

Dante smiled wryly. "The flowers I brought?"

"I shared them with everyone. I still have some issues." Beau avoided saying that if he'd left them in his office, he'd have sneezed all day long. "The thing was, that fall, with the cooler weather, was good for me, and so my dad took me with him. We had found a natural blind, right on one of the deer paths. It was perfect and the woods were so beautiful, all filled with the fall colors. We hunted with bow and arrow because that was when Dad could get time off. Not that it mattered. The trip was all about spending time together."

"My dad never did things like that with me," Dante said softly. "He enrolled me in little league, and I played four years. My dad came to three games the entire time. He always said he was busy...."

"My dad made time for me. At least for a while." Beau swallowed. "I was up in the tree and had a good spot as a group of deer came by. It was perfect and I lined up the shot. I could see the buck's neck right at the end of the arrow and was about to let it go when it happened. I couldn't stop it and began to sneeze. The deer broke into a run and I lost my shot."

"I bet you were angry." Dante met his gaze and held it. "I know I would be."

"Yeah, I was, and I climbed down, continually sneezing.... I checked my pockets and remembered my dad had my meds.

I went searching for him." Beau could no longer look at Dante and sat back, staring ahead. "What I didn't realize was what had really scared the deer. It wasn't me, but a large black bear. He was interested in filling his belly one more time before winter, and at that moment, I looked like a snack."

"Oh God," Dante whispered.

"I yelled at the top of my lungs and tried to make myself as big as I could. The bear stood on its hind legs, cried out, and then attacked." Beau shivered as the car grew arctic cold in seconds. "I remember being clawed and going down to the ground, figuring I was going to die. The pain was so bad, and all I could do was say goodbye in my head and wait for the end to come. I heard shots, and that was all I remember. Dad had a pistol with him, which he apparently emptied into the bear."

"Holy crap."

"Yeah. Dad did first aid and called for help. I don't remember a lot of it because I was in and out, but they took me out by helicopter. It's the only time I ever got to ride in one, and I don't remember anything about it. I spent months in the hospital. They treated the wounds, which became infected, and it was pretty nasty because it spread. I had to have surgery in order to repair the damage once they cleared out the infection, so…." He looked down. "I'm not pretty and I never will be. I know that."

"Beau—"

"I know who I am, Dante. After the attack, I had amazing people who worked with me to help me accept my limitations. The infection affected my kidneys some, as well as my lungs. I'll never be able to run a marathon or do heavy, taxing exercise. I have to watch some foods, and I drink in very small amounts. I also don't go to the beach or run around without a shirt. That's just the way it is." Beau shrugged. "The people who helped me accept who I am also made me want to become a counselor so that I could help people."

"Why alcohol and drugs?" Dante asked.

"Because that's where I was needed, so it's where I went. I love working with the kids, and there's very little in life more satisfying than watching as someone figures out their way in life and puts themselves on the path to true happiness. It sometimes takes years, and it's never easy, but when it happens, it's so gratifying to know that you really helped someone." The car slowed down, and Beau leaned to peer out the window. "Is this the turnoff?"

"Probably," Dante answered, moving closer to him once again. Beau tensed as Dante looked like he was going to kiss him again. "What's wrong?"

"You don't need to feel like you have to do this," Beau told him. "I know I just told you a lot about what happened to me, but I didn't do it to make you feel sorry for me."

"Has that happened to you before?"

"Yeah. I had a boyfriend a few years ago. At least I thought he was. We'd dated for a month and things were getting physical, so I told him about myself. He said it didn't matter, only it did once I took off my shirt. Well… he wasn't ready. I saw him go pale and then turn away. I let him off the hook and told him I was tired. He took the excuse, and I never heard from him again."

"So you expect everyone to act that way?" Dante asked softly, with a hint of confusion.

"Like I said, I don't have any illusions that guys are going to ultimately find me attractive, and I can live with that." Beau had worked through his body issues years ago. He really had made peace with who he was and had figured out some time ago that he wasn't likely to meet someone who could look past the scarred body. "I basically like who I am and have no delusions about the person I am."

"Then if that's true, why did you ask me out to dinner that afternoon?" Dante's eyes danced, and Beau felt them probing for some sort of deception.

"I thought you might need a friend. I didn't expect anything more… not really. Like I already told you, there was something about you that perplexed me, and not many people do that." Beau shrugged. "I certainly didn't anticipate flowers or being whisked away in a limousine for dinner. And quite frankly, I don't expect anything happening after we eat." His cheeks heated once again, and he glanced away, looking out the window as they passed through the outskirts of the lovely little fishing and tourist town. "I definitely didn't anticipate to be kissed within an inch of my life beforehand."

"You assume that every man you meet is so shallow that they can't look past the outside?"

Dante leaned forward, and Beau felt breath on his neck. He purposely didn't turn around even as heat raced through him. He wanted to believe that was possible, but it wasn't likely to be anyone as stunning as Dante Bartholomew. He also doubted that anyone hurting as Dante seemed to be would be able to open himself up like that and accept what was on the inside.

"I don't expect it, but I think it's pretty much inevitable. I can live with it." Even as the words crossed his lips, he wondered if they were true. Had he really thought that he would be alone all his life?

"Would you turn around?" Dante asked, and Beau shifted slowly in his seat, meeting Dante's gaze. "It seems a shame to cut yourself off from everyone like that."

Beau raised his eyebrows. "Why? You seem to have done just that. Are you happy?"

Dante sighed. "I don't think I'm meant to be happy. I think the decisions I've made have made it impossible and made me unworthy to be happy."

The car pulled to a stop, and Beau reached to open the door. "How about we continue this conversation later?" He stepped out of the car and waited for Dante.

"We'll be a few hours. I'll call you when we're ready to be picked up," Dante told Juan, who nodded and pulled the limousine down the street. Dante motioned to the small restaurant, and Beau climbed the steps to what had once been a grand Victorian home and was now a luxurious restaurant with scents to boggle the mind wafting through it.

"Wow," Beau couldn't help murmuring as he glanced all around and inhaled slowly, letting the warmth of spicy herbs, a touch of garlic, and a hint of heat encircle him.

Dante spoke to the hostess, and then they were escorted through the richly decorated space filled with glorious antiques to a table in the base of the round tower that jutted above them into the night.

"This is really nice." He hadn't imagined Dante would make a reservation at the best restaurant on the Eastern shore.

"I hoped you'd like it." Dante took his seat, and when the server came over, he introduced himself and took their drink orders. Dante ordered a bottle of sparkling wine, as well as bottled water. Then they took a look at their menus.

Beau was completely torn. Everything sounded amazing, and he had no idea what to choose. Eventually he settled on a strawberry-laced salad to go with fresh snapper. Dante ordered sea bass and a Caesar salad. He thanked the server and waited for him to leave.

"Have you ever been here before?" Beau asked.

Dante nodded, a cloud passing over his face. "This was Allison's favorite restaurant."

"Do you think that's a little strange?"

Dante shrugged. "I remembered the restaurant and asked Roberts to make the reservation. I didn't give it much thought until I got here."

"We can go if you need to."

"No." Dante sat straighter in his chair. "It's been a long time."

Beau thought a second. "What was she like?"

"Allison?" Dante seemed shocked.

"Yeah. What was she like?" Beau hoped getting Dante to talk about her would make things easier.

"She was my best friend. I met her in the ninth grade, and we became friends very quickly. My dad liked that I had a girlfriend, even though we were only friends and nothing more. Her family used to go on these long, huge vacations every summer, and the last few years of high school, they took me along with them. We went out West and saw all the national parks. Stuff like that. We stayed friends through college, and then once we got out, I went to work for my dad, and she went on to study law and eventually worked for a big law firm in DC."

"But did you know you were gay?"

"Yes, and so did Allison. That's why we became such close friends. There wasn't a bunch of sexual tension between us. We loved each other and helped look out for each other. Allison was a great friend." The cloud of darkness washed over his features once again. "Anyway, she had a great sense of humor—at least she did when we were kids. As we got older, she got more serious and put herself through law school. She was very determined and dedicated to her career for a while. But apparently she lost interest. That was Allison all over. Even as a kid, she threw herself into things and then grew tired of them after a while. She moved back to St. Giles and opened her own legal practice because she said she wanted to help the people there."

"Is that when you grew closer again?"

Dante nodded, and the server arrived with a champagne bucket on a stand and opened the bottle, poured their glasses, and then left them alone once again. Beau wanted to ask some more questions about Allison, but it seemed Dante had said all he wanted to say, as his expression hardened.

"This was her favorite restaurant, and we used to come here a lot when we were first married."

Beau was glad he'd been wrong, and if Dante wanted to talk, he'd let him.

"What are you doing here?" a man growled, and Beau turned his gaze from Dante to a tall, broad man standing next to their table. He stared at Dante, mouth curled in a sneer. "You aren't fit to be seen in public with anyone, you fucking monster."

Every head in the restaurant turned their way, and their server scrambled over. "Sir, you need to leave." The server called for others as the man continued to glare at Dante.

"I know what you did, and so help me, I will make you pay for it." The man leaned down, lowering his voice. "I've hated you for years for what you did to Allison. I'm not afraid of you. I will make you pay for what you did. The law might have let you off, but I won't." He straightened up and jerked away from the servers. Then his glare shifted to Beau, growing icier by the second, sending a bone-deep chill of pure hatred through Beau. "Is this what you replaced my sister with? A man?" His lip curled upward, and Dante got to his feet, seemingly ready to stand between them.

"Sir, either you leave or we will call the police." The server sounded unsure of himself, but the message seemed to get through.

The man turned away from the table, storming toward the door as rage washed off him like water over a precipice. He banged a table near the entrance, sending it toppling, glassware shattering and silverware jangling as it hit the floor. He didn't even pause, slamming the door behind him.

"I'm sorry, sir…," the server began.

"It's all right," Dante said as he drew himself up to his full height and sat as regally as possible. Beau knew it was a front, but one Dante had to put on in order to somehow rise above what had just happened.

"Who was that?"

"Harper Bledsoe, Allison's brother. As you can tell, like everyone else, he blames me for what happened to Allison." Dante met Beau's eyes. "And I can't blame him. I didn't murder her, but I am responsible for what happened." He lowered his gaze to the table.

"Do you want to go?" Beau asked, placing his hand on Dante's.

"No." Dante shook his head slightly. "I want to have a nice dinner here with you, and then we can take a walk through town and out to the bay. It's pretty here, and you deserve a nice dinner."

Beau could almost see Dante pulling away from him. The time they'd spent together had been strange, but Beau had felt Dante beginning to open up to him. He suspected Dante never talked about Allison to anyone.

Thankfully, most people in the restaurant had returned to their meals. With the excitement over, things seemingly returned to normal. The server brought their salads, and Beau ate and tried to think of something to talk about.

"Next week I have to travel for a while. I've been putting this trip off and I can't any longer."

"How long will you be away?" Beau asked, then took a small bite of his salad, the sweet of the berries and tang of the dressing mixing to perfection.

"A few weeks." Dante smiled. "If you could get away, I'd take you with me. Have you seen Paris and London?"

"No. I haven't traveled a great deal. Not since…." He looked down.

"The attack?"

"Yeah. My dad blamed himself for what happened, and he had some difficult times after that. He drank more than he should and tried to make it up to me. Not that it was his fault. I know that, but I blamed him for a bit too, and that hurt him pretty badly. It took both of us a while to figure things out, but by then I think things had changed between us forever." Beau set down his fork. "But I was wrong. It wasn't my dad's fault. He didn't somehow convince the bear to attack me. It happened."

"What was different afterward?" Dante asked after swallowing, and Beau hesitated. It was hard putting things into words that others would understand.

"You mean after we'd both realized it wasn't his fault?" Beau asked, and Dante nodded. "Time. Lots of wasted time. I was eighteen and could finally see things somewhat clearly. My dad and mom had spent much of what they had on doctors and therapists to help me build up my strength. The injuries on the outside are what can be seen, but the infection had done more damage. Once I let go of all the hurt and hate that I'd let fester, I wasn't the same person, and neither was he. I look back on it now and realize it was such a waste."

"Your father is still alive, isn't he?"

"Yes. And we have a better relationship now." Beau sighed. "Let's talk about happier things, okay?" He turned to look out the window and could see the bay in the distance. It was smooth, and the sun sparkled off the water.

"Yes." Dante ate a little faster. "My dad used to keep a boat moored here, and we'd go out fishing sometimes. Mostly we'd just ride. He loved going fast, the sensation of speed. It was never something I liked. But sometimes it was such fun, with the bay quiet, and when he'd open up that engine, it felt like we were flying across the water."

"Before the accident, my family was hugely into the outdoors. I told you about hunting, but we used to camp and went hiking a lot. For one vacation we rented a cabin at a lake, and it came with a small boat that had a motor on it. Dad let me drive it, and we went all around that lake." Beau smiled and turned away to wipe his eyes. "I think it was that summer that things between him and me really started to heal." He used his napkin to wipe his mouth and nearly gasped at the naked pain in Dante's eyes. Beau had gotten a second chance with his father once he'd allowed himself to let go of the blame. Dante had never gotten that kind of second chance, and Beau suspected that was what he was seeing at the moment. "Somehow we always seem to circle around to the same things." He needed to lighten the mood. Beau smiled as the darkness eased from Dante's eyes.

"What do you suggest?"

"Let me see. I like long walks on the beach, hiking in the woods, being on the water—though I burn really fast so I have to wear a gallon of sunscreen to be out there—and I love a good cheeseburger that's dripping with onions." Beau grinned. "If I was to try online dating, that would be my profile."

"You're goofy," Dante told him, but his lips curled upward, and that was the reaction Beau had been going for. "Okay. Let me think. If I was to go for online dating… I like traveling and seeing new things, food of all kinds. I'm really experimental." Dante leaned forward. "I like quiet evenings at home, reading, a warm fire in the winter, and I'd really like to get a dog." He sighed. "If I was being honest, I always hoped I'd be able to have children and a big family." Now he was getting back into dangerous territory.

"That's not a surprise, with the way the kids at the Center reacted to you. Would you come back in once you get back from your trip?" Beau finished his salad, and the server took the dishes, then brought their main dishes, which were works of art on a plate, the scent of heaven wafting through the air.

"I definitely will." There was the smile that could light up a room, and it sent the surge of heat racing through Beau that it always did. He was becoming addicted to those smiles, and he somehow needed to break that habit. Dante was carrying so much hurt and pain around with him that getting his hopes up was a surefire way to get himself hurt. But Beau hadn't figured out how to do that.

"What else?" Beau took his first bite, groaning in near total delight. He looked up from his food as Dante shuddered, and Beau realized Dante hadn't moved to start eating.

"You shouldn't make sounds like that," Dante whispered. "They make me want things I know I shouldn't have."

"Why not?" Beau challenged, lifting his eyebrows. "You wear your past around you like an anchor, and I know you don't think you can let it go, but you're the only one who can. No one else can take that away or let you live your life going forward."

"No one is going to let go of the past. Not in St. Giles."

Beau didn't argue and took another bite, groaning just a little louder. He was teasing Dante, and it seemed to be working. He gaped as Beau deliberately lifted another morsel of fish to his lips, biting it slowly, watching as tiny beads of sweat broke out on Dante's forehead. That was beautiful and a bit of a shock to Beau. Dante really liked him, and Beau's heart did a little jump of joy.

"Man, you're being mean, you know that?"

Beau swallowed and took another bite. "Or am I being beastly?"

Dante snorted. "That was really bad…." His words ended in a groan as Beau gently licked the back of his fork. "What are you doing?"

"You act like nothing affects you. In a crowd, you stand away like you're afraid you'll hurt someone. Most of the time you're afraid to go out, and you've pretty much cut yourself off." Beau smiled. "To top all that off, you and I have one thing in common— neither of us ever thought we'd find love. Am I right?"

"Yeah." Dante stilled his hand as Beau reached for another bite of fish. "Do you have a point?"

"I think it's ironic, and kind of hot, that you're going crazy watching me eat." Beau grinned. It sure warmed his heart.

"So what do you want me to say?" Dante leaned over the table. "That I think about you most nights and find it hard to go to sleep and end up picturing your eyes? When I'm supposed to be working, I can't concentrate and wonder what your lips taste like? Is that what you want me to say?"

Beau swallowed hard, and it had nothing at all to do with the food. "What I want from you is the truth and for you to stop living in the past. You deserve to be loved, just the same as everyone else."

Dante sat back in his seat. "I'm not sure if that's true. I believe that our actions have consequences, and if that's true, then maybe the result of my actions should be that I end up alone. Maybe that's my punishment." He returned to his meal, eating in silence.

Beau thought the silence should bother him, but it didn't, and the meal was so amazingly flavorful that his own plate pulled his attention. "Someday you're going to have to tell me what it is that's got itself wrapped so tightly around you." Beau kept his voice as gentle as possible.

"What if I'm never ready?" Dante took a final bite and set down his fork on his nearly empty plate.

"Then that's something you're going to have to decide about. You can't have your secrets and what you're so afraid of as well as love and lifelong companionship. Secrets have a way of growing and festering like a wound." Beau waved a hand in the air, considering his next words. "Think about some of those things you said you wanted. You can't do them alone, you know. So what's more important to you, holding on to the past or trying to move forward? I know what those answers are for me, but I can't answer them for you. Only you can do that." He sat back as the server cleared the dishes and placed a dessert menu in front of each of them.

"Would either of you like any coffee?"

"No, thank you," Beau answered, then waited while Dante declined as well. "Are you having dessert?" Beau loved sweets, and the menu appeared completely decadent, with crème brûlée, a mint and chocolate creation that the next table seemed to be enjoying, and a strawberry and vanilla parfait that had his stomach rumbling even though he'd just eaten a rather large dinner.

"I'm not sure. We could share one."

"The mint one?" Beau asked, and Dante's eyes broadened and he inclined his head just a little. When the server returned, Dante placed their order, with two spoons, and soon a beautiful plate with a chocolate cylinder filled with mint mousse and whipped cream was set between them on the table. The gentle scent hinted at the lusciousness to come. Beau didn't want to be the first to break the artistry on a plate. Dante, thankfully, took the first bite, and then he had one.

"I told you about those sounds." The touch of growl in Dante's voice sent a shiver through him.

"But it's so good."

"And if you do that teasing thing with your spoon again, I'm not going to be able to restrain myself, and I don't think the restaurant would welcome us back if….” Dante let the repercussions hang in the air, and Beau's imagination went into overdrive. Dante's eyes darkened even more, and Beau wondered what kind of kettle of fish he'd just opened. A zing of arousal raced through him, followed by caution. He'd been through this before, and that memory acted like a wet blanket.

Dante might have been flirting with him, but that was all it was likely to be, no matter what his bedroom eyes screamed at him. Once Dante accepted who he was and let go of his past, he could have any guy he wanted at any time, and he wasn't going to want… well, once he fully saw what was under Beau's shirt, he wasn't likely to stick around. Hell, he'd already found out that very little killed the mood faster than his body once he took off his shirt.

“Dante.” He tried to add a note of caution, but Dante seemed to take it completely differently. He took another bite of the dessert, and it must have been Dante's turn to tease, the tip of his tongue making an appearance, and Beau couldn't help wondering what Dante could do with it if he decided to take the chance.

Oh hell… two can play this game.

Beau teased right back until he heard a female voice from the next table.

“I'll have what they're having.”

He tried to suppress his chuckle and saw Dante doing the same. Then he turned and winked at her. The lady appeared to be in her sixties, with beautifully coiffed hair and a glint in her eye that was adorable. She reminded Beau of his own grandmother, who had passed away when he was a teenager.

“That'll teach you,” Beau told Dante.

“I wasn't the one who started it, but I could finish it.”

Beau leaned over the table once again, keeping his voice low. “I dare you.” He was feeling bold. After all, what did he really have to lose? Beau already knew what rejection felt like, and if Dante couldn't take it, then….

"What are you thinking about? It must be really naughty." Dante's voice wrapped around Beau like a pair of strong, sweaty arms around his bare chest.

Beau shrugged. He had no intention of mentioning that if anyone could take the way he looked, it would be the Beast of St. Giles, and at the moment, Beau was up for some of the Beast. It had been a long time since anyone had made his heart race faster and faster the way Dante did. So if the opportunity presented itself, he'd be a fool to pass it up.

He took the last bite of dessert, still gazing at Dante, who stared back with the heat of a volcano. Suddenly the air-conditioned restaurant seemed hot as the very depths of hell. The server brought the check, and Dante paid the bill before Beau could ask about his share. Then they were on their feet and walking out into the night air, pervaded with the scent of water.

"Do you want to take a walk?" Dante asked, and to Beau's surprise and delight, he took his hand, guiding him down the main street of town. Most of the small tourist shops were closed, but their windows glittered with displays of glass and estate jewelry, even amber. "The waterfront is this way."

They walked down the wooden walkway toward the docks but stopped as a huge yacht slowly glided out toward the bay. "I'd love to spend time on something like that. Not that I ever will, but could you imagine leaving port, heading down the coast in that kind of luxury, and ending up on some tropical island with palm trees, sand, sun, and nothing to do but make love all day and…?" Beau stopped as he realized he was going on like an idiot. He stood still as the water lapped at the pilings under the dock.

The last of the sunshine faded fast as they watched, with more and more lights flicking on, glinting and dancing on the water. Boats moved in and out, their lights like red and green lanterns gliding through the darkness.

"This is beautiful," Beau breathed, and Dante squeezed his hand. He'd grown quiet, and Beau was a little concerned until the cool breeze blew in off the water and Dante shifted behind him, wrapping Beau in his arms. An arctic gale wasn't going to chill him as long as Dante did that.

"Yes, it is."

Beau angled his head and shoulders and saw Dante looking at him rather than the view all around them.

"Hey, Beast!" The call popped the bubble of contentment around them. "Yeah, I'm talking to you."

Beau groaned as Dante pulled away. They both turned as Harper, the man from the restaurant, charged toward them.

"That's enough!" Beau snapped. "I've had it with people using that name! I don't know what happened with your sister, but this is not the time or the place." He curled his lips at the strong sharpness of alcohol that leeched from Harper's pores. "Go home and sleep it off before you do something you'll regret." Beau took two steps forward, hands on his hips. "I mean it." He'd had to deal with more than one drunk person in his career.

"But he…." Harper's resolve weakened, and some sort of sense seemed to percolate through his alcoholic haze.

"It doesn't matter. I will call the police, and then you'll be arrested and that will be more trouble." Beau held Harper's rummy gaze for as long as he could. "Go on home," he added more gently. "You need to get some sleep anyway. It's all you really want right now, isn't it?"

Harper nodded and yawned.

"Go on and walk home." Beau continued making himself appear as large as possible, and the last of the fight in Harper slipped away. He turned and lumbered off into the night. "Well, that was certainly interesting."

"Holy crap," Dante breathed from behind him. "Do you have Jedi powers or are you the drunk whisperer?"

"Neither. The guy is basically a coward. There was no real fight in his eyes, and as soon as I called him on it, he folded like a house of cards. Once he did, all I needed to do was remind him of what his body wanted anyway. Alcohol is a depressant. His system was slowing down, and once I planted the idea, it was going to take root pretty quickly."

"I see."

"Besides, no matter what anyone thinks of you or what you might have done, calling people names is no way to behave. He should know better. Calling others names is just a way of trying to put yourself above someone else. No one gets to do that. I don't allow it in the Center or any of my sessions, and I certainly won't let some drunk get away with it, no matter who he is." Beau breathed deeply as the adrenaline-induced racing of his heart subsided.

"I see." Dante grinned. "So you'll be my protector."

"Not that you need one." As his mind cleared, he realized how dumb he'd probably looked. Dante could certainly take care of himself. After all, he was definitely bigger and could stand up for himself. It was just that the man's tone had gotten to Beau in a way that set him off.

"It's been a long time since anyone stood up for me." Dante seemed genuinely shocked.

"Then it's about fucking time," Beau said with more vehemence than he initially intended. He turned back toward the water, letting its calmness work its way into him once again.

"Are you ready to go?" Dante asked, and when Beau nodded, he stepped away. Beau heard him call Juan and then they walked up to the drive where the limousine pulled up. They climbed inside, and it glided away and back toward St. Giles.

CHAPTER 5

BEAU SAT quietly in his seat while Dante did the same, glancing at Beau every few seconds. Dang, he was a real spitfire. The energy and courage it took to stand up to Harper had been unexpected. What bothered Dante was how quiet Beau had gotten. He wasn't sure what to do to make him more comfortable. Maybe he needed a few minutes to get his thoughts together? Dante was at a loss, to say the least.

"We should be in St. Giles soon." It was lame, but he needed to break the silence.

Beau turned to face him, and the heat that had simmered and spiked all evening took a leap of epic proportions. "If I overstepped—"

"You have got to be kidding." The words tumbled out of Dante's mouth. "You were magnificent, eyes blazing. You reminded me of one of those Scottish warriors charging into the guns, come hell or high water. It was pretty amazing."

Dante leaned forward to speak briefly with Juan and then sat back once again, unable to keep from watching Beau and the way he worried his lower lip with his teeth. God, he was adorable, and knowing there was a tiger inside made Beau even hotter. The things Dante wanted at that very moment he knew he shouldn't contemplate, but the pull was too great. He leaned in, and when Beau met his gaze, Dante guided him closer, erasing the distance between them.

As soon as Beau's lips touched his again, something inside Dante's brain snapped. Years of denial and the realization that Beau was exactly what he'd been missing all that time sent a wave of desire running through him with the force of a racehorse. The car bumped over the road, but instead of breaking them apart,

Dante held Beau tighter. He felt perfect in his arms, fitting him as though Beau were made to settle against his chest. Dante deepened the kiss, his tongue dueling with Beau's, sending more and faster spikes of heat surging through him.

"Dante, I want—" Beau said, and Dante kissed him again, Beau returning it with everything he had. Nothing mattered as long as Beau was in his arms, and Dante didn't even realize the limousine had stopped until Beau pulled away and his mind began working once again.

"I guess we're here," Beau whispered and opened the door. He climbed out, stumbling once and using the side of the limo to steady himself. Dante loved that he was able to affect Beau that way, and when he was out of the car, Dante wrapped an arm around Beau's shoulder to guide him toward the front door, where Roberts waited silently. Dante didn't pause as they passed, taking Beau to the living room.

Beau didn't sit down, instead gently rocking from foot to foot. "What did you have planned?"

"I hadn't given it much thought. I—" Dante didn't get a chance to finish. In seconds he had his arms full of Beau. Then they were kissing, and Beau damn near tried to climb him. Dante held him tightly and did his best not to fall over and bring both of them to the floor.

Dante's mind had pretty much shut down by the time he started moving them out of the room and toward the stairs. Beau stumbled on the first step, and Dante caught him, their gazes meeting, filled with heat. "Are you sure about this?" Dante asked.

"That's my question." Beau placed his hand on Dante's chest, the warmth searing right through his shirt. "It's going to hurt if…."

"I understand." Dante guided Beau up the stairs, holding his hand. He was on fire and his hand shook with energy. He paused outside his bedroom door, letting Beau make the final decision about what he wanted. Dante wasn't going to push him and had to know Beau was okay with what was going to happen. What surprised him was the way Beau opened the door, stepped into his bedroom, then tugged Dante inside and kicked the door closed.

Beau turned around, gazing so deeply into Dante's eyes, he could almost swear that Beau could see to his soul and was able to read all his secrets. It chilled him, until Beau wrapped his arms around his neck. If Beau did know what he held in so tightly, what he was afraid to let out, it didn't seem to bother him. Of course he didn't know, but Beau gave him the impression that no matter what he kept hidden, it was okay for now. That was enough for Dante.

He closed the distance between them, and when their lips touched, Dante slid his hands up Beau's side and under his shirt, feeling slightly bumpy but hot skin under his palms. Beau shivered. Dante slid his hands upward, bringing the shirt along. He pulled his lips away and tugged Beau's shirt over his head, then dropped it to the floor.

Beau worked the buttons of Dante's shirt and slid it off his shoulder. He stepped back and raked over him, licking his lips. "Jesus…."

"What?"

"The night I first met you, I tried to imagine what you looked like under that tuxedo, but my imagination was sorely lacking." Beau closed the distance between them, pressing against Dante, probably in a bid to hide his own chest from view. Dante knew Beau was reticent about being seen and let him remain obscured, especially with the way he ran his hands over Dante's shoulders and down his arms, then over his chest, sending heat searing through him and deep into his heart.

Dante quivered from the energy, kissing Beau again in order to give the building passion an outlet. He slowly guided Beau back toward the bed, lowered him, and followed him onto the thick duvet, working open his pants and sliding them down his quivering legs.

Beau stilled, and Dante knew what was behind it. "You need to let go and trust me," Dante whispered. He'd already felt the scars, at least some of them. He knew they were there, and the roughness had tickled his fingers.

Beau inhaled sharply. "Do you know how hard it is to expose yourself to someone, let them see all of you, good or bad? It's scary as hell, and once I do, you can't unsee it, no matter how much I might want that."

"It's the same for everyone."

Beau hesitated a second. "No, it isn't." He turned away, covering himself.

"All right." Dante kicked off his shoes, then glanced over his shoulders. Beau sat hidden under the duvet, holding it up over himself. Dante stood and slipped off his pants and then his boxers, standing naked in front of Beau. "This is me."

Beau's eyes boggled and he gasped. "Wow." The adoration was sexy as hell, and Dante groaned as his cock, already pointing toward the ceiling, throbbed as he moved closer to Beau.

"What do you want?" Dante asked quietly, breathily, as he climbed on the bed and crawled closer to Beau, who hadn't moved a muscle except to pant slightly. "Go ahead and lie down."

Once Beau lay back, Dante kissed him hard, taking possession of his mouth, showing him as best he could just how much he wanted him.

"Dante," Beau groaned, and Dante took the opportunity to suck lightly at the base of his neck before slowly sliding his lips down Beau's shoulder. All the while he kept Beau occupied, Dante tugged the duvet lower and lower, following it with his lips.

Beau gasped, and Dante sat back. Scars crisscrossed Beau's chest and down his belly. They were white now from age, but still visible. Dante hadn't honestly known how he'd feel once he saw them, but all that came to mind was the pain and agony that Beau must have endured.

"See… I told you they weren't pretty."

Dante lightly traced one of the most pronounced scars near the center of Beau's chest down to just above his navel. "These are part of you. If you got these in battle, would they bother you as much? They're war wounds, and it must have taken all the strength in the world to endure what you did." He leaned forward to lightly kiss one of the scars.

Beau quivered under him, panting for breath, so Dante did it again, then gently licked the white line as Beau nearly went to pieces. "God, that's…. Why are you doing that?"

"These are part of you," Dante answered. He wasn't going to let Beau think he was ugly. These scars were strength, courage, and a test of endurance. All of those qualities were unbelievably sexy on their own, but together, they were mind-blowing.

Dante shifted back, tugging the duvet off Beau completely. He saw the worry in Beau's eyes, like a swirling mass of blackness, but he ignored it, hoping he could replace that with light. Instead, Dante shifted his gaze to Beau's long legs and then up to his thighs and hips. He leaned closer once again to suck a mark at the dip just inside his pelvis.

"Dante," Beau groaned with a combination of laughter and pleasure that sent a zing straight to Dante's cock. He continued upward, ignoring Beau's long, thick cock for the moment. He had more important organs to attend to, and the one that was important right now was the one beating inside Beau's chest. The scars became more numerous, and he stroked along them, the roughness sliding under the pads of his fingers. Beau squirmed a little.

"Does this hurt?"

"It's tickly, but not painful." Beau shivered and closed his eyes.

"Don't try to hide or escape, please." Dante wanted all of Beau present in this moment. Once his deep blue eyes opened again, the worry he'd seen earlier had been replaced with what Dante could only describe as hope. He paused, seeing that gleaming at him, and closed his own eyes, wondering if he could dare let that hope inside him. He'd closed it off for so long—was it possible to allow it inside him once again? Dante darted forward, slamming their lips together, taking what he needed in that moment.

When he pulled back because he needed to breathe, Beau wrapped his arms over his chest protectively.

Dante shook his head, gently took hold of Beau's wrists, and brought them over his head. "Hold them there."

Beau quivered under him. "What are you doing?"

"Proving you're wrong." Dante kissed Beau once again, then trailed his tongue down his neck to the longest scar, licking a line down it to just above Beau's belly button, the rich, manly taste of Beau building on his tongue. He swirled his tongue in the shallow divot, earning a gentle chuckle that shifted to a groan as Dante slowly licked and sucked his way back up.

"Why are you doing this?" Beau breathed.

"Because you need to understand that the guy, whoever he was, was a damn fool." Dante flicked his tongue around one of Beau's nipples, and he whined softly, so Dante did it again, sucking the tiny bud to a peak and worrying it with his tongue. "They're only scars."

He closed his eyes once again and held his breath. "I told you…," Beau began. "It's too much."

It took Dante a second to realize what Beau was talking about. "No. It's not you. They're not you." Dante pushed the impending realization aside. He could deal with that later. Right now, it was all about Beau, and Dante sucked at his nipple once again while he traced the scar that ran just alongside it.

"How can you do that?" Beau groaned.

Dante lifted his gaze, meeting Beau's. "Because these are part of you. These scars, these marks aren't just yours any longer. They're mine. I'm tracing them, putting my mark on top of them."

"You're what…? Claiming me somehow?"

"Yes!" Dante hissed. "I'm claiming you. I'm the Beast of St. Giles, and I'm claiming you and taking what I want. You've driven me to distraction for weeks, and I want you. All of you. Can you understand that?" He held still, waiting for Beau's reaction. All he received was a nod, and then Beau swallowed. Dante had the answer he needed, and he kissed his way down the lightly furred

90

trail beneath Beau's belly button to the treasure he found there, then sucked Beau's girth between his lips.

"Oh *God*!" Beau cried, and Dante took more of him, sliding his lips down the shaft as Beau's heady richness burst across his tongue. It took control Dante hadn't needed since he was a teenager for him not to come right at that moment.

He sucked Beau hard, letting his hands roam up and down Beau's chest and belly, needing Beau to know Dante accepted him for who he was.

Beau flexed his hips, sliding his cock across Dante's lips and tongue. It was glorious, and he closed his lips tighter, loving that Beau quivered under him. Beau carded his fingers through Dante's hair, tugging on it lightly as Dante used his mouth to drive Beau nearly out of his mind. Dante felt Beau's control beginning to slip, so he revved up his pace, bringing Beau just to the edge before backing off.

"Dante…." Beau moaned, his entire body going rigid as his cock throbbed and bounced against his belly. "You're fucking mean."

Dante yanked open the drawer of the bedside table, his own control perilously close to the edge. He nearly dropped the drawer to the floor before locating a silver packet and ripping it with his teeth. "No… not mean." He leaned forward. "But unless you tell me to stop now, I intend to go ahead and fuck you. I need to feel you around me." He could barely hold still long enough for Beau to whisper a *yes* into his ear. Every instinct he had urged him forward, his last shreds of control fraying by the second.

Somehow he had to not lose it now. Beau deserved care. Dante took deep breaths to calm the rages of passion while sliding his knees under Beau's legs, lifting them upward. Fucking hell, Beau was limber, and Dante gasped as Beau tugged his knees to his chest, exposing his most private opening to Dante's heated gaze. He leaned forward, tracing his finger along Beau's crack, teasing the puckered skin of his opening before sucking his way down Beau's inner thigh, bringing his lips closer and closer to Beau's opening as he shook harder and harder in near-breathless anticipation.

"What are you doing to me?" Beau pleaded as Dante licked over Beau's opening.

"Getting you ready," Dante answered, then buried his face between Beau's cheeks, supporting his hips with his hands until Beau quivered uncontrollably. There were few things in life—that Dante had seen, anyway—that compared to Beau in the throes of anticipatory joy. Dante pulled away, taking in the sight presented to him. Beau's eyes were huge and his mouth hung open, chest heaving with each breath. He moved his lips but didn't manage to say anything for a few seconds.

"I'm ready…," Beau gasped and pressed his hips forward.

Dante swore this man would test the patience of a saint. His instincts told him to go for what he wanted, and he was seconds away from it, but he had to be safe for both of them. Dante searched the bedding and found the stupid packet among the folds of the blanket. He rolled the lubed condom down his length, then pressed into position, his gaze locking onto Beau's. He pressed forward, slowly, Beau's body opening to him.

"Is this too fast?" Dante asked, stopping as he breached Beau's body.

"Hell no." Beau reached for his leg to pull him closer, and Dante let go, sinking deeper into Beau's searing heat.

Dante caught his breath, waiting for Beau's body to accept him, then slowly began to move. He didn't want to hurt Beau, and every move sent waves of heat and energy through him. He held himself back, remaining in control.

"What are you waiting for?" Beau demanded, pulling Dante down until their lips were just an inch apart. "I'm not going to break. So show me how you're feeling right now."

"I won't hurt you."

"I'm not made of glass. So fuck me like you mean it!" Beau crashed his lips to Dante's, and his control slipped away.

Dante closed his eyes as his desire took over his entire being. Dante understood lust—he'd felt it many times over his life—but the glimmer of love and the deep connection he seemed to have with Beau was completely new and added to the experience. More than anything, he wanted Beau to be happy. He snapped his hips, the entire bed rocking slightly under his force.

"Yes!" Beau encouraged, and the last of Dante's self-restraint shattered. He saw red for a second, then rocked back and forth, driving deep into Beau's heat, withdrawing, and then shaking as Beau took him over and over again. Everything around him—hell, his entire world—narrowed to Beau and only Beau. The entire house could have fallen down around him and he wouldn't have known it or cared. All he wanted was right here with him at that moment.

"Fuck me!" Beau cried, pulling Dante out of his head and back to Beau, who yanked him down into a kiss that sent a shudder running through him.

"Damn, you look...." Words failed him completely. Beau stretched out under him, long and lean, gasping softly as Dante slid deep, holding still. He had always heard that there was a difference between sex and making love, and he'd never understood that. But he did now.

When he was married, he'd loved Allison, but in a completely different way from how Beau seemed to touch his soul. He could barely think now, and let go of everything running through his head. Dante gathered Beau to him, holding him tightly as they rocked together until the last of Dante's control snapped.

Beau came unglued around him, crying out softly, and Dante followed right behind him, emptying himself, his vision narrowing to the passion on Beau's face.

Slowly Dante came back to himself, withdrew from Beau and took care of both of them before joining him on the bed once again. He pulled Beau to him, settling with his chest pressed to Beau's back. "Are you all right? I can barely move." He was sated, worn out, and as happy as he could remember being.

A knock sounded on the door, and Dante groaned, pulling up the covers to make sure Beau was hidden from anyone's gaze. Then he got out of bed, slipped on a robe, and cracked the door open. "What is it, Roberts?" he asked though the small opening.

"I wasn't sure if I should disturb you and Mr. Beau, but Mr. Yates is downstairs, pacing the hallway like a cat. We told him that you were occupied and had gone up to bed for the night, but he's most insistent."

Dante yawned and wanted to tell Simon to go and come back at a decent hour, but his lawyer wasn't the type of person to panic or overreact, so he pulled the robe closed around himself. "Tell him I'll be down in a few minutes." He shut the door and turned back to the bed.

Beau sat on the edge and already had his pants in his hands. "I should go and let you take care of whatever you need to."

Dante strode over to sit next to him. "I don't know what he wants, but I'll take care of everything as quickly as I can and come back." He leaned close. "I don't want you to leave." Hell, his possessiveness had kicked in, and if he could help it, he'd never let Beau out of his sight. But it was way too soon to say things like that and not sound demented.

"Are you sure?" Beau asked.

"Definitely," Dante told him and pressed Beau back down onto the bed. "I'll be looking forward to the best sight I've ever seen—you here in my bed." He kissed Beau and then, reluctantly, got up and made sure the robe was secure before leaving the bedroom and descending the stairs.

"Simon, what couldn't wait until morning?" He wasn't happy being pulled away from Beau.

"I've been trying to get in touch with you for hours. You probably need to check your cell phone and make sure it's charged." Yates opened his bag and pulled out some papers. "You're being sued for wrongful termination by the union."

"You interrupted me for that?" Dante snatched the papers. "This ass was stealing from us and we can prove it. There was no wrongful termination. I didn't use that reason to spare his family, but if he can't be man enough to tell them the truth, then I certainly will." He paced the front hall, stomping hard enough on the floor to rattle the nearby table. "Some people have all the nerve in the world."

"What do you want me to do?" Yates asked. "I knew you'd want to know as soon as possible."

Dante cleared his head. This wasn't Yates's fault. He was just the messenger, and Dante did want to know as soon as possible. "Come on." He padded to his office and opened the lower desk drawer on the left to pull out one of the files. "Here is the documentation you need. Contact them and present the facts to their attorney. If Greg wishes to pursue this, we'll press charges, and Greg will go to jail. I'm not going to play around with this any longer. I've had picketers at my house, and all for someone who embezzled from us."

Yates seemed pleased. "Is there anything else?"

"Yes. If he decides to pursue this, I want a judge to order him a psych evaluation. I'm willing to bet there's something wrong with him. No sane person would act the way he has."

"I don't know if we can do that."

Dante lowered his gaze. "Just bring it up. Use whatever you have to in order to get Greg to let this drop. I don't want to spend more money defending myself when we've already lost enough because of this asshole. Hell, he's using my own money to try to sue me." Dante had already spent enough time and effort on him. Now he was trying to make up the losses they'd suffered.

"All right. I'll get on this first thing in the morning."

"Is there anything else?" Dante stood. "If not, I'm going up to bed."

"Dante," Beau said softly, and he turned toward the door. His first instinct was to hurry over to stand between Beau and Yates. Beau had on a pair of shorts and one of his T-shirts, and he looked totally edible.

"I'm on my way." Dante turned to Yates, who was already closing his bag and getting ready to leave.

"I'll take care of everything." Yates's face was beet red. "I didn't realize that you had company." He hurried out of the office, and Dante heard Roberts tell him good night, and then the front door opened and thunked closed. Roberts had the good sense not to return, and Dante met Beau at the office doorway, turned out the light, and took Beau's hand.

"Is everything okay?" Beau stroked the back of his hand, easing away some of the tension.

"Just a continuation of the protestors the other night. Hopefully we've put an end to this now." As they climbed the stairs, Dante sighed. "I want to go over to Greg's house and rip his head right off his shoulders. That asshole steals from me and then tries to sue me when I fire him. I should have called the police and let them deal with it." He gripped the banister, stopping just before the top of the stairs. "I was trying to be a good guy and…. Shit. I should have just stepped back and let things take their course."

"It's over, isn't it?" Beau asked.

"God, I hope so. I told Yates to throw everything we have at him. Scare the shit out of him and he'll go away, and hopefully take his family along with him." Dante started up the stairs again. "I know they think they're standing up for him, but Greg hasn't had the guts to tell them what he did, and now they blame me for what happened. Everyone blames me for everything."

Beau tugged on his arm, and Dante stopped. "Self-pity isn't becoming," Beau told him. Dante half expected him to smile as though he'd been teasing, but he didn't. "You say everyone blames you for everything, and yet you do nothing about it. You carry all this guilt and expect everyone to look past it. They can't until you do." Beau tugged him forward. "Come on. It's getting late and you have a bunch of things you need to do in the morning, I'm sure. I have to be to the Center early so I can catch up on the paperwork that makes the world go around."

Dante wanted to argue with him, but as he thought about it, there was nothing to argue about. Beau was right. He had been grousing over self-pity, and danged if Beau hadn't refused to put up with it, but called him on it. That should have made him angry, but instead he drew Beau to him and hugged him close. Here was one person who wasn't afraid, intimidated, or willing to tell him what he wanted to hear. His father had always said that he'd fallen in love with Dante's mother because she didn't take his bullshit and saw him for who he was.

"Are you angry at me?" Beau asked as they reached the bedroom door.

"How can I be angry when you're right? Sometimes I may growl about it, but you have a way of cutting to the heart of things. It may piss me off, but it's refreshing too."

"Good." Beau rose on his tiptoes and gave him a kiss. "Because I have a feeling that I'm going to be right quite often and you should probably get used to it."

"You do, huh?" Dante said, trying to be playful.

Beau paused and then seemed to make up his mind. "Yeah. I know you're used to being right and having people come to you for decisions, and once you make up your mind, that's pretty much it… and you get pissed as hell when your wishes aren't carried out."

Dante narrowed his gaze. "How do you know that?" There was a definite growl in his voice that he tried to suppress.

"It's not rocket science," Beau said with a shake of his head. "You generally get what you want and you're used to it."

"Yeah, but no one listens to me." After all, who wanted to spend time listening to the Beast? They simply dealt with him when they had to and stayed away at other times.

Beau went into the bedroom, began taking off what little he was wearing, and then slipped into bed. "I think you have things messed up. Everyone listens to you. How can they not? You have control over half the town, including the biggest employer. The problem is that no one likes you—there's a difference. It's hard to like someone you're scared half to death of. People in town stay out of your way, talk about you behind your back. You know they've made up stories about you because you hear them."

This wasn't the kind of conversation he expected to have after he and Beau had just made love. "I see."

Beau lifted the covers, and Dante hesitated before dropping his robe and getting in bed with him. "But they don't see the real you. It's too deeply hidden. The people around you here do and they stay, and you let me see some of what's under that steel exterior of yours and I like you. The kids do too." He ran a hand over Dante's belly, and flutters of renewed desire beat in his chest. Beau reached over to turn out the light on his side of the bed.

"Aren't you going to tell me what I should do?" Dante asked as he turned off his light, plunging the room into darkness.

"Nope. That's up to you to decide." Beau settled next to him and gently rubbed his cheek until Dante turned his head. Then Beau kissed him hard, demanding, and just like that, the desire that had been building burst to renewed flame once again. Before Dante could move, Beau had shifted, climbing on top of him, kissing him deeply enough that he felt it in his soul. "For now it's time to stop thinking about beasts and what everyone else thinks." Beau sucked at the base of his neck, and Dante groaned, stretching to give Beau better access. "Because what really matters right now is what I think." He licked down Dante's chest to his nipple, then teased it before pausing. "And I think that we're both going to be tired in the morning."

And Dante had no argument for that.

THREE DAYS later Dante woke from a dozing sleep, high above the Atlantic. He looked around and stifled the groan that rose to his lips. He knew he had no right to, but he missed Beau. They'd spent an entire night together, just one night, and Dante had never been so tired in the morning, or so thrillingly happy. Now once again he was alone.

The flight attendant made her way up the aisle and inquired if he needed anything. Dante quietly asked for some water and closed his eyes once again, trying to sleep and return to that dream he'd been having where Beau had just walked into his office, closed the door, and somehow all his clothes had vanished by the time he'd reached Dante's desk. In the dream, Beau was unblemished, no scars, with perfect… well, everything, and eyes that radiated heat and desire.

Dante opened his eyes again, the hum of the jet engines intruding on his thoughts. Was that what he wanted? Beau to be perfect? He thought about it and realized he didn't see Beau as anything but beautiful, scars or not. And that scared the hell out of him. Beau was perfect. He was generous, caring, understanding, and seemed to be willing to put up with him.

And that was the problem. Dante knew he didn't deserve anyone like Beau.

"Sir, your water," the flight attendant said, and Dante took the cold bottle, thanked her, and tried to get comfortable in his business-class seat once more. He pulled the blanket up over himself, closed his eyes, and hoped to hell he'd be able to go to sleep.

Allison was there in the house, standing at the top of the stairs, smiling as brightly as she always had, no hint of the sadness that had been building inside her, adding to the lines around her eyes for the last year and a half. She was the Allison he knew, his best friend, the person he'd loved for years. The one person he'd always been able to confide in.

Dante rushed over to her, and before his eyes, she aged and her eyes grew hollow and cold. With each step, she turned into the person she'd been at the end.

Allison fell toward the stairs. Dante leaped to reach her, his hands grabbing, but she remained just out of reach. "This is your fault. You did this to me." Her words rang in his head as she disappeared from sight. Dante didn't need to come closer and look to know what he'd find. He'd already seen that image in his head, burned into his memory forever.

Dante jerked upright once again, nearly toppling the bottle of water on the little armrest tray. The other passengers were all shifting, waking up, and having breakfast before the flight crew prepared the cabin for their landing in Paris. Dante hoped the dream would fade, but it didn't seem to, and even after they'd landed and Dante was getting off the plane, the image of Allison, aged and drawn, lingered in his mind.

FOR THE next week, Dante struggled to keep his thoughts on the business at hand. He made a number of deals in Paris that would benefit the business greatly, and some of their art pieces even won an award at a salon. But none of that managed to banish the constant thoughts of Beau during the day and then the dreams and nightmares of Allison at night. Over and over, Allison went to her death, and each and every time, she blamed him. Not that Dante had any illusions—her death was all his fault. It just hurt like hell to have it play over and over again in his head.

He made it to the station just in time for his train, boarded, and took his first-class seat, then ignored the scenery outside the window as the train barreled through the French countryside on its way toward the Channel that it would travel under.

His phone vibrated in his pocket and he answered it, checking the time. He had a little bit before he lost the signal. "Bonjour."

"Dante?" Beau said tentatively.

"Yes, it's me." He smiled because he couldn't stop himself. "I'm on the train from Paris to London, so we'll get cut off once it enters the Channel."

"Are you having a good trip?" Beau asked. "Did you get done what you hoped?"

"Yes. We won a gold medal at the Porcelain Salon. I can't wait to present it to Florian Cindersen when I get back. He's the head designer for our decorative line. Maybe I'll have him to the house so you can meet him."

"Is this a big deal?"

"Huge." Dante worked up some enthusiasm. He knew he should be over the moon. That award would mean that they'd get orders from all over the world for years to come.

"Then have a reception for him. I can help you plan it if you like." Just like that, Beau was there to try to help.

"That would be nice. I'll think about what we want to do. Maybe a celebration for the entire division." Dante yawned. He was getting very tired of traveling, though he still had a week or more to go. "What's going on there? Are you doing okay?"

"The Center is busy. Bobby asked when you were coming back. I think he's thinking of ice cream. Even Kendra grudgingly admitted that you weren't mean—it's a long story—and asked if you were coming back." Beau sighed. "I want you to come back. I know we haven't been… whatever we are for long, but I miss you. I almost called you my boyfriend, but I wasn't sure if that's what you wanted to be, and…."

"Of course, I'd be honored to be your boyfriend." Dante wasn't so sure if Beau would want that once he found out about his past. His phone beeped to indicate that he'd lost the signal, and Dante stared at the screen, wondering what Beau had heard or not heard. He shut down his phone and shoved it back into his pocket. More than anything he needed to get his head screwed on straight and make some decisions before he could allow things between them to get any more serious.

Dante's heart was already engaged, and that was part of what concerned him the most. Beau deserved to know the truth about his past. That much he'd decided. The fallout to his heart was a completely different matter.

ANDREW GREY

He returned Beau's call once the train emerged from the Channel, but it went to voicemail. Dante left a quick message and ended the call, then rode in silence for the rest of the trip. He took a taxi to his hotel from Victoria Station and settled in for the night. With his mind made up on a course of action moving forward, his dreams were quiet and he was able to sleep for the first time in weeks.

102

CHAPTER 6

"YOU'RE SERIOUS? Mayor Grant wants to speak to me?" Beau asked Angie when she gave him the message. He'd been on the phone with Dante when the call had come in.

"Yes. That's what Shirley said. I took down the number for you." Angie continued with her work, her usual enthusiasm sorely and obviously absent. "I put those grant applications on your desk for review before I send them out."

"What's going on?" Beau perched on the edge of her desk, which she absolutely hated but Beau knew was a way to get her to spill the beans.

"The town received an offer for the Center from a developer," Angie said. "It was brought up at the council meeting last night, and Gertrude Lawson called me this morning to tell me all about it. I didn't put much faith in it because Gerty doesn't get a whole lot right, but apparently the amount of money being offered is more than the town can afford to pass up."

Beau's shoulders slumped. He turned back toward his office and picked up the phone to return the call.

"Mayor Grant's office."

"This is Beau Clarity returning his call." Beau sat down, his leg bouncing with nervous energy.

"Yes. Mr. Clarity. The mayor is on another call, but would it be all right if he stopped by the Center in an hour? He needs to speak to you."

"At least he's got the guts to deliver bad news in person," Beau said, and Shirley didn't correct him, which was telling as far as he was concerned. "I'll be here and available."

"Thank you." She ended the call, and Beau settled the receiver in the cradle and tried to return to his work, but his mind refused to settle. It wouldn't. When he'd taken this job, he'd been assured that the community and the town had been behind the Center and the programs he'd taken on.

THE PHONE on his desk rang and he answered it.

"Beau, the mayor is here."

"I'll be right out." He took a deep breath, left his office, and headed down to get the bad news.

"Mr. Clarity," Mayor Grant said, stepping forward in his suit and tie, looking sharp and extremely businesslike.

"Mayor Grant, what can I do for you?" Beau shook his hand.

"Is there somewhere we can talk?" Mayor Grant asked, and Beau motioned toward one of the counseling rooms, then followed behind and closed the door after them.

"I'm aware there's some sort of offer that's been made on this building," Beau said, cutting to the chase. "Is the town really considering selling the building and closing the Center? There's a real need for the services we're providing, and the building is all the funding the town supplies."

Mayor Grant raised his hand, and Beau stopped. "I'm well aware of the amazing job you and your staff are doing here and that you raise your own money and don't require an ongoing line in the town's budget. But St. Giles isn't in the real estate business, and we've been offered enough money for this building to allow us to do a number of community upgrades that we've been searching for the resources for over the last five years."

"So what? You and the council made promises when you hired me, and those promises will be kept. The Center and its continued functioning were among those. You yourself told me that the community was behind the Center, as was the town council.

104

You don't get to lie to me that way." Beau crossed his arms over his chest, his fists clenched tight.

"We are behind the Center and your programs, and we'll find a new location for you, but the town council is seriously considering accepting the offer on this property." Mayor Grant reached for the door. "I thought it best to tell you in person rather than just letting the council act on the sale." He seemed so damned smug. Beau's stomach trembled.

"You do realize that my next step will be to go to the newspaper here in town, as well as the Annapolis and Baltimore news organizations? This is going to be a great human-interest story, and I will play it up to the hilt. So the council members and you had better be ready for some serious questions, because they're going to be coming at you." Beau grinned. "And when the reporters do come, I'll have a group of seven-year-olds meet them." He was so angry, he wanted to smack the smugness off the mayor's face. Mayor Grant swallowed hard, and Beau stepped forward. "This Center provides a great deal of value to the community and you know it." He now understood why Dante thought Mayor Grant was less than useful.

"As I said, we will work to help find another location. But you have to understand that this offer is too good for anyone to pass up." Mayor Grant looked around the room. "This facility needs a large number of upgrades, and the building itself is at the end of its useful life. The Center, as well as the town, is spending more and more on maintenance." He reached for the handle. "We need to work together to find a solution that will work for everyone." He opened the door and strode across the hallway to the Center's front entrance, pulled it open, and stepped outside.

As soon as the door closed behind Mayor Grant, Beau swore under his breath and stomped back to his office, slumped into his chair, and put his head in his hands. Beau knew he could make arguments until he was blue in the face and Mayor Grant and council would still do whatever they wanted. Sure, he could raise a stink, but it wasn't likely to change anything. He was a new person in town and had little say.

Honestly, Beau stared at the phone. His instinct was to call Dante to see if he could help, but he was in London and it was now late enough that hopefully Dante was in bed getting some rest. No, this was something he needed to try to handle on his own. No matter how he felt for Dante, or how Dante might feel for him, he wasn't going to use those feelings to try to get something he couldn't get for himself.

He called down to the desk. "Can you come see me as soon as you can?"

"Give me a few minutes," Angie told him, and Beau hung up and did his best to get through the rest of the work on his desk. A few moments later, Angie knocked and came in. "Was it as bad as I thought?"

"Yes. The useless weasel." Beau placed his hands flat on the desk. "But we aren't going to take this lying down."

"We're going to fight?" she asked, rubbing her hands together.

"You better believe it. Find out how much the offer on the building is and who's making it. We should also get in touch with all of our clients and their families. Tell them what's happening. Try to get them to come to the next council meeting. We need to show support for the Center or we aren't going to have it."

"Okay. I'll see what I can find out." She left his office, and Beau stared at the wall across from his desk. He hoped to hell that Dante was having a good trip, because Beau's ability to possibly have a week where he wasn't worried about something had just flown out the window.

He missed Dante and had wanted to call him all the damn time, but he had to restrain himself. Dante was working. But damn, he just wanted to hear his voice. Beau hadn't anticipated just how much he could come to miss the gruffness, power, and heat in Dante's voice after such a short time.

"You know," Angie said from his doorway, and Beau jumped a little. He hadn't been expecting her to come back, and damn, that

woman could walk like a cat sometimes. "You could call Dante...."
She lilted her voice when she said his name.

"I could. But I'm not going to. This Center is important to the community and to all the people we help. But if we can't make our own case for it—and I'm willing to fight tooth and nail, by God—if the community doesn't care enough to keep it, then what the hell are we doing?" He looked up from the papers he'd just set back down. "We need to mobilize the community to support us and find out who it is we're up against." And he wasn't above finding out what their weaknesses were either.

Angie grinned. "There it is. That's the fighting spirit." She turned, and Beau sighed. He had to get through this damned paperwork, but his mind wasn't on it. He needed to get on the ball or there would be nothing to be doing paperwork for.

THE FOLLOWING afternoon, after they had composed emails and sent them to everyone on their mailing list explaining the support and show of numbers they needed and when the next council meeting was going to be held, Angie burst into his office and closed the door. "I found it." She plopped herself into the chair with a self-satisfied look in her eyes.

"Okay. What did you find?" Beau was checking his email, and his belly turned for the millionth time. It was empty and remained that way. He had hoped to receive a flurry of calls and emails expressing outrage and support, but so far there had been nothing from any of the clients they serviced.

"Are you with me?" Angie asked, and Beau focused his attention. "So, I went to the diner and had coffee, sitting with Mrs. Arenson and her crowd. I drank enough coffee this morning to float a battleship, but I heard nothing, not a blessed thing." She grabbed one of the files off his desk and fanned herself with it. Beau laced his fingers and waited. There was no rushing her when she was like this. Beau had learned he needed to let her say what she wanted to or, heaven help him, she'd start over. "They were about to leave when Mrs. A finally said that it was a shame about the Center."

"So word has gotten around."

She rolled her eyes. "Of course it has. We sent out, like, a million emails. My inbox is loaded with responses and people ready to show up at the council meeting." She shook her head as though he was an idiot. "I gave them the main Center email, remember?"

Beau wiped a hand over his forehead. That was a relief.

"And I got the paper to do a story on the Center and what closing it will mean. We're going to kick some ass, Beau. But, look, as I was saying, I had coffee with Mrs. A and the ladies and I got nothing until Mrs. A said that it was a shame about the Center." Angie paused for effect. "Then she added that the whole thing was Bartholomew's fault."

Beau blinked a few times and leaned forward. "Is Dante buying the building?" That couldn't be right. Dante knew how important the Center was, and he'd never do that. But a speck of doubt made his belly churn.

"No." Angie lightly smacked his hand. "Just listen okay? Mrs. A said that it was all Dante's fault because the guy buying the building is Harper Bledsoe. Who knows how much of this is right. But Mrs. A said that Harper saw you and Dante out together, and the word around town is that you are seeing each other." Angie barely stopped long enough to take a breath and then spoke lightning fast. "There are two camps about that in town. One is that you better be careful in case the Beast decides to do to you what he did to his wife. The other is that maybe if Dante has someone in his life, he'll be easier to get along with. Everyone worries about you because you're such a 'nice young man.'"

Beau's head was throbbing. "Can you get back on track?"

"Yeah. Anyway, I'll save you the details, but it seems they think that Harper wants to build a small retail center, and this is one of the locations he was looking at. He picked this one because…."

Beau sighed. "He could have his center and get at Dante through me somehow."

"That's what I heard. Doesn't mean it's true, of course, but I was able to talk to Shirley in the mayor's office, and she told me that it is Bledsoe who's made the offer."

"Where did he get the money?" Beau wondered out loud.

Angie shrugged. "Does this help?"

Beau groaned. "I don't know. Yeah, he has some motive, whatever that may be. And all this about Dante could just be the gossips putting stuff together and coming up with the most salacious things possible."

Angie nodded. "That's true, and I won't argue with you. But at least we know who we're up against."

"Yeah." Beau groaned and closed his eyes, knowing in his heart that him seeing Dante had just complicated their lives and put the Center in danger. Not that Beau intended to let that affect things between them. But it did point to the fact that whatever had happened with Allison, and all those secrets, was now about to affect the Community Center and the people he helped. Beau had no idea what he was going to do about it, except fight the purchase with everything he had.

"Do you know Mr. Bledsoe?" The few run-ins Beau had had with him hadn't left a good taste in his mouth.

"Not really. Some people in town do. He grew up just outside St. Giles and went to school here for a while." She scratched her forehead like she was trying to remember something. "I saw him a few times. He moved to St. Michaels about the time that the Be… I mean, Dante got married. I understand Harper and Allison had a really rough time of it." She leaned forward a little. "I know their parents died a year after Allison did. They were close as far as I know."

"And now Harper is a big-shot developer? He must have been smart or lucky to have made enough money to do what he's planning."

Angie chuckled. "He got it from his sister, apparently. Rumor had it that Allison bought a lot of life insurance and made her brother the beneficiary. So when she died, he got a lot of cash." She sighed. "This is rumor talking here, and I don't know how much faith to put in it, but that's where he got the cash to start his business, and by all accounts, he's a really good developer, well respected. He won the contract to rebuild the waterfront docks in St. Michaels. They're beautiful, with those little shops that are small enough and inexpensive enough that small businesspeople and artists can afford them to sell their work. We could use something like that here."

"Angie, please…." Beau was getting a headache from all her tangents.

"Okay, okay. The point is, Bledsoe got a pile of money because of his sister's death, and it looks like he's using some of that to try to buy the Center."

"All to punish Dante through me because he saw the two of us together?" Beau knew that was a stretch. "There has to be more to it than that."

"Oh, there probably is, but I don't know if we'll ever figure out what it is. That reason may be known only to him right now. But if you want, I can try to do some digging."

Beau groaned. He wasn't sure what to do. "Sure, go ahead, but we have to be careful of all privacy concerns. I don't want anything that might pertain to the Center or our work to make it into the realm of the rumor mill. But if you can find something out, bring it to me and no one else," he said, deadly serious. The last thing he wanted was any of the Center's records and practices being called into question. Right now it was only a fight for the Center's building and not for the very survival of the organization.

"Of course. I never talk about anything at the Center outside these walls." She seemed almost affronted. "Why do you want to know?"

"Because as much as I hate to"—especially after the confrontations he'd already witnessed—"I might have to try to meet with him and see if we can work things out." That idea was a last resort. His best chance was to put enough pressure on the council and Mayor Grant to get them to back off the sale. "Let me know what you find out." Beau checked the time and stood. "I need to get to a session with the kids."

"All right." She left the office, and Beau went on down to the kid-friendly area to get it ready.

"How are things going?" Dante asked when he called that evening. It had to be well after midnight in Europe.

"Pretty good. I told the kids you'd be back to visit when you got home, and they were really excited." Beau kept the issue regarding the building to himself for now. "How much longer before you come home?"

"I'll be there Friday night, and I thought we could have dinner on Saturday. It's been a great trip, but I'm looking forward to seeing you." Dante hesitated. "There are some things I think I need to tell you." Dante's voice grew softer, and even through a transatlantic connection, Beau could hear the worry.

"Just come home in one piece, and I'm looking forward to seeing you too. We can talk about whatever you want once you get here and have had a chance to rest." He was so looking forward to seeing Dante and having him back. He'd lived a quiet life for a long time, and now that he had someone to share it with, or the beginnings… maybe, sort of… of someone in his life, he wanted them close.

"I will." Dante yawned, and Beau told him to get some rest. Then he ended the call and tried to get his mind back on what he needed to.

His phone chirped with a message from Angie. *Special council meeting next week to discuss sale. Wednesday @ 7:00. Will get message ready to go out tomorrow. Let's mobilize the troops.*

He answered her and then finished his dinner before settling on the sofa to rest and try to chill out.

The days inched by. Parents and other clients all asked about what was going to happen to the Center whenever they came in, and the entire staff reassured them as best they could before encouraging them to show up at the meeting. A lot of people said they would, but Beau knew agreeing to show up and actually making an appearance were two different matters.

By the time Friday arrived, Beau was on pins and needles. Dante texted him when he landed at Dulles and let him know that he was on his way to St. Giles, but the drive would take a few hours.

Do you want me to come see you? Beau texted back when Dante said he was just crossing the Bay Bridge a few hours later, which meant he was ten minutes or so away. It was after eight, and Beau had just finished eating a light dinner and had settled on the sofa.

His text went unanswered for a few minutes, but then his phone dinged. *I'll be out front in five.*

Beau sat up and looked around for his shoes. His heart rate grew faster as the seconds ticked by. He hadn't expected to go out, not really, and he needed to clean up. He hurried to the bathroom, washed as quickly as he could, brushed his teeth, and changed his shirt, ready for Dante when he arrived out front.

The back door of the limousine opened as Beau approached, and he climbed inside, pulling the door closed. He was immediately tugged down onto the seat. No words were spoken, but that was probably because Dante pulled him into a kiss that left Beau breathless, and he loved every second of it. His week had been horrendous, but it was immediately better now, with the tension melting away, replaced with a different kind of energy that thrummed through him in the best way possible.

"God, I missed you," Dante whispered.

"Me too." Beau sat back, not looking away from Dante as he recommitted his taste and the way his eyes darkened to memory once again. Beau still found it hard to believe that someone like Dante would find him attractive. But one thing he told the people he tried to help was to accept and enjoy the good things when they came, and he was determined to do that. "But your trip was worthwhile?"

Dante nodded. "I'll tell you all about it, I promise." He tugged Beau closer as the car pulled out and they glided through town. Dante kissed him again, and for a little while, Beau let go and just felt. It was what he needed right now. "Usually I love my trips overseas. No one there knows me as anything other than Dante, and there are no other expectations or pressures other than business. But this one was different." Dante smiled. "I've never had someone to come home to before."

Beau swallowed hard, closing his eyes, trying to decide if he wanted to ask the question that popped into his head. "What about with Allison?" He braced for Dante to pull away, but he held still, then tightened his hold on him.

"She was my wife, but we were more like friends than anything else. At least that's how I looked at things. I traveled when I needed to, and she had her own life and activities. Well, that's how I thought things were between us. That was the agreement we had when we arranged to marry." Dante sighed softly. "While I was away, I decided to tell you about her and what happened between us. But I don't want to do that tonight. I don't have the energy or the patience for that right now."

"I can understand that." The car bounced and tilted slightly as they pulled into the driveway of Dante's estate.

"Thank you, Juan," Dante said through a break in the partition and then opened the door. He climbed out, not letting go of Beau's hand, and led him through into the house, where Roberts met them in the hall. "When do you need to work tomorrow?" Dante asked.

"I have a session at eleven."

Dante turned to Roberts. "We'll have breakfast at nine."

"Very good. I'll arrange to have the luggage brought in, and I'll take care of it in the morning so you aren't disturbed."

Dante nodded, and Beau smiled. "I appreciate your care." He liked knowing that when he wasn't around, someone watched out for Dante, even if that's what he was paid to do.

Roberts didn't seem to know what to say to that and nodded carefully. "You both have a good night." He turned to leave the room as Dante tugged Beau up the stairs.

"I don't think anyone has ever left him speechless before." Dante sounded pleased.

"He does take care of you and looks after you all the time. And I don't think a lot of what he does is really his job." Beau paused at the top of the stairs. "I mean, does he ever sleep? He'll make sure the luggage is inside and the dirty clothes in the laundry. He'll lock up the house and check that it's secure. Then he'll go to bed and somehow he'll be up in the morning before either of us to ensure that you have everything you need." Beau stroked Dante's cheek. "I know you see what people do around you, but sometimes you maybe take them for granted."

"I don't," Dante said quietly. "I'm well aware of how lost I'd be without him. Hell, there have been times when I thought he was the only person I had in my corner."

Beau nodded gently. It wasn't his place to offer an opinion, and he'd probably already said too much on the subject. Not that he had strong disagreements.

Dante squeezed his hand and led him to his bedroom, pushed open the door, and stepped inside. He turned on the light beside the bed, the single bulb casting a gentle glow through the room.

"Do you need to clean up?"

Dante removed his jacket, laying it over the back of one of the chairs, and unbuttoned his shirt. "Yes. I've been cooped up in planes and cars for hours." Shirtless, his skin glistening, Dante pulled him into a tight embrace. "How about you join me?" He yawned, which told Beau a great deal about just how tired Dante was and that it was likely that sleep was going to be the only activity happening in the bed.

"Go ahead and shower. I'll ask Roberts about something light to eat, and then we can get you in bed." Dante needed someone to care for him at the moment; the dark circles under his eyes told Beau that. He stroked Dante's arm, the muscles rippling under his touch, weariness seeping into Dante, making his shoulders slump.

Beau left the room and found Roberts downstairs, taking care of the luggage. "Is there something light to eat?"

"Of course." Roberts put the bag he was carrying next to the stairs. "I'll bring something up in a few minutes if that's all right." He retrieved the second suitcase and closed the front door.

"Beau." Dante's voice drifted down the stairs. No bellow or harshness, just need and bone-weariness.

"I'll be right up," Beau answered, then turned back to Roberts just in time to see him nod and hear a soft sigh. Beau raised his eyebrows in curiosity, but Roberts said nothing more, so Beau climbed the stairs. He found Dante in his room, naked, sitting on the edge of the bed, half-asleep.

Beau started the shower for him and got Dante moving into the bathroom. He heard the sound of the water change when Dante got in the shower and waited for him to finish. Roberts knocked on the door, and Beau took the tray with a few rolls and some ham and cheese on it, along with a pot of what smelled like chamomile tea, and set it on the dresser.

The water sound didn't change, so Beau peeked into the bathroom to find Dante mostly asleep under the water. Beau slipped off his clothes and climbed into the shower with him, lathered his hands, and soaped Dante's broad back.

Dante jerked as soon as Beau touched him.

"It's all right." Beau continued lathering and then stepped closer, pressing his chest to Dante's back and his hips to his butt, letting his hands roam over Dante's chest.

A rumbling sigh rolled through the enclosure, and Dante lolled his head back onto Beau's shoulder. He continued soaping, his fingers gliding over taut skin and hard muscles. He made no effort to entice or tease. This wasn't about sex or lust, but care and gentleness. It was about being close and sharing an intimacy that in some ways was more personal than sex. About taking care, showing support, and looking out for the other. Beau also knew it was something even more than that. It was the Beast, his Beast, Dante, a man who had to be strong for everyone, letting Beau take care of him.

Beau washed Dante's hair and then pressed him forward, the water running over both of them. Once the traces of soap and shampoo had slid away, he turned off the water and grabbed one of the huge, soft towels from the counter. "Go ahead and dry yourself," Beau said softly as he did the same. "There's food and tea out in the bedroom."

"God, I had no idea how long this trip was going to feel."

Dante dried himself mechanically and most likely on instinct. Beau hung up the towels when they were done and guided Dante to the bedroom and down into one of the chairs. He pressed a roll with ham and cheese slices on it into Dante's hands, and he ate automatically, drinking some tea.

Beau sat in the other chair, eating a few bites himself. What surprised him was that he wasn't self-conscious and hadn't thought about how he looked or about the scars that ran down his chest. When Dante lifted his gaze, there was nothing in it but happiness and banked want and heat. Beau had always thought he'd come to terms with what had happened, but in those few minutes, he realized he'd now made the final step on that very long journey. If Dante didn't care about those scars and what they looked like, then why should he? Beau didn't see himself going shirtless on a beach anytime soon, but he was done worrying about the disfigurement.

"Let's get you into bed." Beau took the empty cup, placed it on the tray along with his own, and took Dante's hand to guide him to the bed and under the covers. Dante rolled over away from the light and settled immediately. Beau got into bed, turned out the light, and snuggled into the warmth. Behind him, Dante muttered something under his breath and then, with what had to have been the last of Dante's conscious thought before he fell asleep, he tugged Beau closer and wrapped his arm around him. "Good night," Beau whispered.

Dante muttered something in return and then his breathing evened out and he was asleep. Beau stayed awake a little longer, wondering what Dante was going to tell him in the morning and how Beau was going to impart his own news.

"BEAU," DANTE said, cutting into the glorious dream Beau was having of being next to a pool and Dante sliding his lips…. "It's after eight."

"Oh." Beau rubbed his eyes and sat up, the bedding pooling across his hips. "I didn't know I was that tired." He slid out of the bed and trudged to the bathroom to take care of business before returning to the bedroom. Dante lay on top of the covers, hands behind his head, staring at him. Beau looked right back, his gaze raking down Dante's sculpted chest and hard, tawny nipples, along with the rest of him.

"I missed you." Dante opened his arms, and Beau jumped on the bed, to Dante's laughter, those strong arms closing around him. Beau's skin tingled wherever he touched Dante, and when their lips met, the fire that had been smoldering deep inside since Dante had picked him up last night burst into open flame. He pressed Dante back on the pillows, stretching out on top of him, kissing Dante with everything he had.

"I thought of you all the time." Beau ground his hips against Dante's, the attraction threatening to overwhelm him. Somehow he kept his control enough to enjoy the closeness that had been denied for the last two weeks. "Those were the longest two weeks I can remember." He tilted his head upward slightly, kissing Dante hard, taking what he wanted as his entire body ached with need.

"For me too." Dante guided their lips together, sending a series of overlapping waves of electricity and heat racing through Beau. He quivered and shook as Dante slid his hands down his back to cup his ass with their strength.

Beau stilled and raised his head enough to catch Dante's gaze. "I have to check—don't you have places you need to be?"

Dante shook his head. "Nope. Just right here with you." He caught Beau's lips once again. Beau had to go to the Center, but not for a while, and it wasn't long before thought of anything other than Dante became impossible.

BEAU WAS almost late for his session, but he was more than happy about it. His entire body sang with energy, and he was sore in some pretty wonderful places.

"I take it he's home," Angie quipped as he strode into the Center. "I have your group for the morning in the gathering room at the end of the hall. They were wondering why you weren't here already because you're always so early. I told them you were probably getting busy." She kept a straight face, and Beau waited her out. Angie would say many things, sometimes outrageous stuff, but he didn't believe she'd ever do that.

"He is home, and that's all I'm going to say." Beau flashed a grin.

"Did you tell him about the Center and what's happening? Especially since it looks like he might be the cause of all of this?"

"No. We need to be able to fight our own battles. If the Center is going to survive, then it needs to be because the community is behind it. Not because Dante Bartholomew wants to make his boyfriend happy." Beau tapped the counter twice and then headed down to his group session, which took an hour. Then he went to his office and sat at his desk, trying to compose what he wanted to say to the town council in order to make them understand their case and why it was best that the Center stay where it was.

A knock sounded a few hours later—Beau had no idea where the time went—and he lifted his gaze. Dante filled the doorway, staring intently at him. "What's up?"

"Why didn't you tell me?" Dante demanded.

"About what?" Beau kept his tone as light as he could.

Dante took a step inside the office. "About Harper's offer on the building."

Beau sighed and stood, walked around the desk, and closed the door. "I didn't tell you because it doesn't have anything to do with you. He's made an offer to buy the building, and the town board is considering it. The mayor is all in favor, but I'm hoping to get the community behind saving the Center."

Dante practically growled. "This Center does a hell of a lot of good, and the town knows it." He turned toward Beau. "I will make sure they understand that selling this property is going to cost them a hell of a lot more than what they think they're going to get."

Beau stalked over and jabbed a finger at him. "You will do no such thing." Two could do that growly thing.

Dante's eyes widened and his mouth opened, but nothing came out at first. "Bullshit. I will not allow that to happen."

"And that's why they call you the fucking Beast." Beau was going to do this his way. "The Center serves the entire community. We don't turn people away, and over the years, since well before I arrived, we've helped many hundreds of people. The entire community needs to be behind us, and without them, it would be you deciding what everyone needs. I won't have that. At worst we'll have to find another building, and we may ask for your help then, but this is our fight and we need to be the ones going to battle."

Dante crossed his arms over his chest. "You know that isn't necessary. I can shut this whole thing down."

"Of course I do. But that isn't the way we should be doing things. The town has relied on you and the Foundation for everything. When we wanted a new community pool, they asked you. Beautification project, they came to you. The town needs to fight for what they feel is important, not what you think they should have."

Dante shook his head, scowling. "But this is a stupid idea. Did you find out why they're even considering selling?"

Beau nodded. "The mayor said the building was nearing the end of its life, and I have to agree. We have a ton of maintenance and repair issues every year. The town pays for a lot of those. I don't want to have to find a new space. This one is configured well for us. We would need to put some money into renovations, but we could develop a capital campaign for that."

"Why do you have to do things the hard way?" Dante practically bellowed.

"Because it's the right way," Beau countered. "You know you don't like it when people in town refer to you as the Beast, but you're acting pretty beastly at the moment. Give the people here a chance instead of just swooping in to make the decisions for them. I'm not saying you can't voice your opinion, but that's all." Beau pressed his finger to Dante's chest. "No opening your wallet or making phone calls to pressure folks. That will make them resent the project and your influence."

Dante didn't look convinced. "Okay…," he agreed, obviously reluctant.

"Good. Now, there are some things I think I need to know about what happened and why Harper hates you so much, because apparently the rumor is that he wants the building because he saw you with me." Beau paused. "Look, I can see him having issues with you, and even us. I mean, you were married to his sister, she's gone now, and you're dating a man. He could lash out somehow, and maybe that's what he's doing with the building purchase offer, but I keep thinking there's more to it. And right now, you're the only person who might know."

Dante's expression didn't soften. "I had already decided to tell you what happened. Do you want me to tell you now?"

"No. I'll come to your house after I'm done here." Beau figured it would be better if Dante was comfortable in his surroundings. "This isn't a death sentence, you know." Though Beau would have thought so from Dante's pained expression.

"Have you ever been the cause of someone else's death?" Dante asked with all the seriousness of a funeral director.

"I don't think so."

"Then it's hard for you to understand how I feel. I know what I did and what it did to Allison. I have no illusions about that. But still, talking about it is difficult."

Beau nodded. He understood that. "But getting it off your chest could be exactly what you need." He slowly sat in one of the slightly ragged visitor chairs, and Dante sat in the other. They were so very close, and usually when Dante was this near to him, his temperature rose. "You can't deal with the pain and guilt on your own. You need to let it out so you can work through it."

"Is that what you tell your clients?" Dante sounded skeptical.

"Sometimes. What I do isn't a one-size-fits-all kind of thing. Some people need to talk, and others just need a safe place so they can start to heal. Still others, like the kids you worked with, want attention and a chance to be kids. It's always different, and part of my job is to try to assess what each person might need and how I can try to reach them." Beau met Dante's gaze. "Like with you, every instinct I have is telling me that your story and what happened is pounding at your insides, trying to get out, and you're holding it in so hard that it takes a lot of your energy. That isn't a way for anyone to live."

"You have me all figured out, don't you?" Damn, Dante could be snide when he wanted.

Beau scoffed slightly. "It wasn't hard. You cut part of yourself off and then stayed mostly locked away in that mansion of yours. You shut away what happened with Allison just the same way as you shut yourself away. Our outsides often show what's going on deep inside us, no matter how much we might try to hide it."

Dante didn't dispute him, which Beau thought was a kind of victory in itself. "Okay. Come over after work."

"And talk to Harriet when you get home. Tell her that you and I are cooking dinner tonight." Beau nearly smiled as Dante raised his dark eyebrows. Sometimes he was adorably cute, especially when he wasn't intending to be. "I know that's her domain, but I'm not sitting in that huge dining room, eating at one end of that twelve-foot table like we're in a scene from some Vincent Price horror movie."

Dante rolled his eyes, and Beau stood, leaning over Dante's seat, hands on the arm of the chair.

"Cooking is intimate, or it can be. It isn't just making food. It's textural and sensory, just like what you and I do in bed." He leaned a little closer, just catching the hitch in Dante's breath. "Is that okay?"

Dante nodded once.

"Good. Now I think you better go because I'm about to lean closer to kiss you, and once I do that, it's just a step from tugging off that indecently sexy shirt. And if that happens… well, let's just say that sex on a desk might be something they show in porn, but I don't think it's what I really want to give a try. Especially on this old thing. I might get splinters in my butt, or the danged desk could collapse altogether. Angie would race in here, and I have no intention of letting her see my naked ass on the floor—or yours, for that matter." He leaned just a little closer and then backed away. "I'll see you tonight."

God, Beau loved it when he left Dante speechless. It didn't happen all that often, but when it did, it was pretty special. Beau figured that Dante had thought he'd be quiet and just let him take the lead. That wasn't Beau's style.

Dante stood, and Beau opened the office door. He shuffled out and into the corridor in a slight daze. "You're serious about cooking?" he finally asked.

"Sure." Beau smiled, and Dante left. Beau went back to work, picking up the papers on his desk before setting them back down, breaking into peals of laughter. If the rest of the town knew what a softie Dante could be sometimes….

"What's so funny?" Angie asked, hurrying into the office. "Are you okay? He looked… weird when he left."

"I'm just fine. Now, are we ready for the council meeting?"

"I think so. You need to finish up what you want to say, and as long as the people who promised to support us make an appearance, we should be able to give them a real show of force."

Beau grinned as a thought occurred to him. "Do you know who would be likely to run against our beloved mayor in the next election? Other than Jerry Hansen? Maybe contact them and make sure they're at the meeting. That would certainly put on some pressure."

Angie rubbed her hands together with glee. "Let me put out some feelers. I love making the mayor sweat through his shirts. Somehow we need to stop this."

"We both know the town well enough to know that while they say they'll help us find a new location, there aren't any around that will work. And even if we found one, we'd have to shut down for months while it was renovated to meet what we need... and where is that money supposed to come from?" Beau was already regretting turning down Dante's help—a little, anyway. But he knew he was right. Without community support, the Center didn't matter much.

"I tried looking through town, and the only place that might fit was an old factory building, but it would take more money than we'd ever get to make it useful," Angie said, clearly just as concerned as he was.

"Our best chance is to end this now... at that meeting. So work the phones as best you can, and I'm going to finish drafting my remarks." That was, if he could think straight.

Once Angie left and he tried to get down to work, the words refused to flow. He stared at what he had and tried to think of what he wanted to say, but his head kept returning to Dante and what he could have to tell him. Finally he managed to push Dante out of his head just long enough to finish a coherent draft of his remarks, and then after his final session of the day, he left the Center and went home, where he changed clothes and then got a few things at the store on his drive to Dante's. He rang the bell and was surprised when Dante answered the door himself. "Where's Roberts?" Beau asked as he stepped inside.

"I gave the staff the night off. They deserved some time away from this pile—"

"And that way you wouldn't have to tell Harriet that we planned to use her kitchen." Beau grinned. "I see how it is."

Dante growled under his breath for a second, then rolled his eyes. "I told her we were making our own dinner, and she wasn't too happy until I said that you would be doing most of the cooking. She agreed, apparently because she thought it less likely that you'd set the place on fire." He quirked his lips slightly.

"You didn't…."

"I wanted cookies once, so I made some. Well, I put the frozen-dough kind in the oven. I forgot about them until the entire kitchen filled with black smoke." Dante wasn't laughing.

"You were a kid." At least that's what it sounded like.

"That was last year. I was trying to prove to Harriet that I wasn't a complete menace in the kitchen and ended up making a huge mess. I haven't been allowed in there, unsupervised, since. And to tell the truth, Harriet is too amazing a cook to piss off. So I abide by what she wants."

Beau grinned. "A man will do just about anything to keep his belly full." He leaned close, and Dante kissed him gently before stepping away. "Why don't you lead me to this kitchen so I can put down these groceries and learn where everything is."

Dante closed the door and guided him through to the back of the house and into what could only be described as a gourmet paradise. The counters were granite, with professional stainless-steel appliances and work surfaces. Beau set down the grocery bags and slowly opened each of the cupboards. The kitchen was impeccably organized, with everything exactly where it was needed.

"What are we having?" Dante peered into one of the bags.

"I thought some pasta with pesto and chicken, a Caesar salad, and fruit for dessert. Nothing fancy or too messy, but something we can make ourselves." Beau got out a pot to boil water for the pasta and put the lettuce and salad things on the cutting board. He figured Dante could help with the salad without making too much fuss. Beau found a bowl and placed it near the cutting board, along with a knife.

"Is this what you want me to do?"

"Can you cut the lettuce and talk at the same time?" Beau teased.

Dante didn't smile as Beau made room for him, unpacked the rest of the ingredients, and got out a pan to cook off the chicken. He remained quiet, hoping Dante would want to fill the silence.

"I think I told you that I knew Allison for a long time. She was my best friend for a while and knew I was gay." Dante made a few cuts through the lettuce and then his knife stilled. "She was, like, one of the first people I ever told. And things were good. I was in college, Dartmouth, and Allison stayed here in town. She went to a local college, and I saw her whenever I came home." He kept halting and would cut the lettuce a little more and then stop. The faraway look told Beau that Dante was remembering old times, good ones, at the moment.

"When I came home from college after graduating, the plan was for me to work in the business. I'd done that growing up, and now Dad wanted to groom me to take over for him. That had always been the plan, but he had decided that he wanted me to get married. He wasn't going to let me inherit until I did." Dante brought the knife down hard, splitting the romaine with a solid blow. "Dad never could get used to the fact that I wasn't going to marry a woman and have children. He wanted the line to continue, and that meant I had to get married." Dante's hand shook, and Beau gently reached over, took the knife away, and set it on the side of the cutting board. Maybe sharp implements weren't such a good idea right now.

"I'm fine." Dante picked up the knife once again and returned to his talk while Beau seasoned the chicken and put it in the pan.

125

"You don't look fine," Beau commented gently. He was concerned, especially by the way Dante gripped the knife so hard, his knuckles turned white.

"I wanted my inheritance because I had ideas for the factory. I wanted to restart the artist line. My grandfather had discontinued it, but I knew there was a market for high-quality items as long as they had a more modern feel to them, and I was right." Dante returned to the lettuce, and Beau turned the chicken, letting it continue to brown. He also got the pot of water on for the pasta. "There was no one I wanted to marry. I'm gay and I knew it. So I approached Allison. She hadn't dated anyone in a while, and I knew we got along. She was also struggling under her student loan debt. I figured we'd get married, I could take care of her debts, and after a few years, we'd divorce and move on. I never promised her undying love, but I loved her. She was the closest friend I had at that time, and I thought we'd get along."

Beau had stopped what he was doing to watch Dante raptly.

"I was rather surprised when she told me yes." Dante set down the knife, leaning on the counter.

"She agreed to marry you, knowing you were gay?" Beau asked, checking on the chicken and turning it off to finish cooking through.

"Yeah. She wanted to get away from her mother and father, who had been putting a lot of pressure on her to go to law school. It wasn't something she really wanted, but did to please them, and her family was thrilled at the prospect of the two of us getting married. I didn't tout my sexual orientation, but they all probably thought I'd changed and Allison didn't tell them differently." Dante hung his head. "Looking back, that decision was probably the stupidest thing I have ever done in my life. It cost me my best friend, and I'll never get her back." He gripped the edge of the counter, closing his eyes.

Beau walked to where he stood and slid his arms around his waist, resting gently against his back. "It's all right."

Dante whipped around, and Beau nearly lost his balance. "No, it isn't."

"Did you lie to her? Did you make promises you didn't keep?" Beau asked, staring at Dante, who shook his head slowly. "Did you hold a gun to her head or hurt her physically? Did you murder her?" He had to use those words, harsh as they were, in order to get through to him.

"Of course not," Dante answered.

"Then what happened and why do you think you're responsible for her death?" Beau had to get to the bottom of this. The guilt had weighed on Dante long enough, and he needed to be able to deal with it in the open.

"About a year after we were married…. No, I need to go back further. After we married, I tried my best to be a good husband to her. We traveled and saw a lot of the world. It was so much fun, and we laughed a lot. It seemed like we were going to be happy."

"But that didn't last very long?" Beau asked, and Dante turned away.

"No. We shared a bedroom and slept beside each other, but that was all. I didn't touch her that way because I wasn't interested, and I didn't think she was interested in me that way. I liked having someone to sleep with and having company at night. But after a year or so, Allison grew quiet and began withdrawing. Then my dad passed away, and she grew more and more morose. I took her to a doctor, and they diagnosed her with depression and gave her medication for it. She seemed to get better for a little while after that."

"Did you ever talk to her about getting the divorce so you could each live your lives?"

Dante took a deep breath. "No, I didn't…. She was so down and depressed, and it got worse all the time. I didn't want her to be alone, so I never brought it up. I had brought this mess into our lives, and I tried to do what I could to help her. She got quieter and often tried to initiate sex between the two of us. It wasn't something I was interested in, but she kept trying, and eventually

I moved to the room next door. I think that was some kind of last straw, because she got even quieter and more withdrawn. There were times when she'd stay in her room, in bed, for days at a time. Then she'd come out and act normal, and even happy, for a while, but then the depression would return once more."

"Did you get her help?"

"Yes. I tried, but she fought me on it over and over again. I hired doctors and brought them to the house, but she'd often refuse to see them. My hands were tied, and all I wanted was to have my best friend back."

"Through all of this, you stuck by her?" Beau asked.

"We rode this roller coaster for months, and then in the spring, I had gone away on business for a few days. I had to go. When I got back, she met me at the door, smiling, almost giddy, and said she had something to show me. There was excitement, maybe euphoria, in her eyes. The doctors had told me that the depression could come and go. I asked if she was bipolar, but they didn't think so. She pulled me upstairs, to her room, and pushed me down on the bed. Allison was like a ravenous beast, determined to get what she wanted from me.

"'I want to have a baby,' she told me, and it seemed that night she was determined to start the process. I wasn't interested. After all I'd been through trying to help her, and our years of friendship, being with her… like that… wasn't going to work." Dante lifted his gaze, and his eyes radiated pain, deep and enduring. "I loved her, but not that way. And I think my rejection sent her over the edge."

Beau took the knife from Dante's fingers and placed it on the counter. He was shaking, and the strong man Beau had come to know seemed as vulnerable as one of the kids he worked with. But he wasn't fooled. This door to Dante's vulnerability wasn't going to stay open for long. The walls were still there, just pushed aside. They'd snap back quickly.

"What happened to her?" Beau asked just above a whisper, taking Dante's hands. He needed to maintain as much of a connection with him as possible, as he could feel the resistance building. "Will you show me?"

Dante hesitated, then moved out of the room. Beau held his hand, refusing to let go of him, as Dante led him through the dining room to the ballroom, which was the last place he expected to be taken. The furniture and chandeliers were still draped and the curtains drawn, casting the room with an eerie pall. Light filtered in from breaks in the curtains, illuminating dust motes in shades of red and sunset gold.

"It was late in the day, and I was coming back from work. The house was quiet, silent, and I wondered if something was wrong. No one greeted me, which was strange. Roberts hadn't come to work for me yet. My father's man, Clifton, held that post. I climbed the first stairs to change and heard music that led me to the back of the house." Dante walked almost silently through the room. "Allison was in here, wearing a dress I'd never seen before. It was like she was going to a ball herself. The lights were on and the room was filled with music. But when she looked at me, her eyes were vacant, as though she wasn't really there."

Dante closed his eyes. "I asked her what was going on, and she said that she was having a party. Then she walked over, glass in hand. I wondered how much she'd been drinking. Her wine sloshed in the glass, and she drank what she had before extending her arm. It was like she thought she was handing the glass to someone. It fell to the floor, shattering, and I took Allison's hand. 'Let's get you upstairs,' I said. I led her out of the room." Tears welled in Dante's eyes as Beau let him lead him back into the hall. "I knew something was very wrong. I guided her up the stairs to put her to bed, but at the top, she started fighting me, thrashing and scratching like I was hurting her, but I barely touched her. She screamed at me that I had ruined her. That she loved me and that I had never loved her, not the way she should have been loved." Dante's breath came in gasps as his gaze lifted to the top of the staircase.

"She fell, didn't she?" Beau could almost see it, with Dante staring and shaking.

"Yes. People in town think I pushed her, but I never did. I tried to save her. She hit me, and all I was trying to do was get her to bed. I was going to call the doctor. I lifted her off her feet to carry her to the bedroom, but she thrashed so much, I had to put her down. She screamed that I was going to rape her, hit me, and raced away. I swear she leaped the railing like a gazelle." Tears streaked down Dante's cheeks. "I don't think she realized where she was until she screamed as she flew over the railing right there and knew it was too late. She landed on the floor near where we're standing."

"You never pushed her and only tried to help her," Beau said.

"Of course I did." Dante's voice echoed sharply in the large room. "But that doesn't mean I wasn't the cause of her death. I should have told my father to go to hell. Instead, I married her and made her miserable." Dante pulled away from him. "What happened was my fault. I should have given her what she needed. I should have…." He waved his hand helplessly.

"What should you have done?" Beau looked up at the spot Allison had fallen from. "Not married her, probably. But she knew the arrangement before you got married. Right?"

"Yes. I never lied to her."

"And when you realized there was something wrong, you tried to get help. You even stayed by her when she became withdrawn and erratic." Beau sighed. He'd seen those signs so many times. "Allison was mentally ill. She had a disease. Depression isn't bad moods or being grumpy. It's a medical condition that neither of you could help. It's a disease, the same as cancer or the flu. It isn't a moral failing or something Allison brought on herself. It also isn't anything you did to her or could have saved her from." Beau gently stroked Dante's cheek. Alcohol was also a depressant, and that could very well have made things worse for Allison.

"But I brought this all on."

130

Beau shook his head. "No, you didn't. She most likely had clinical depression before you were ever married. She was ill. Did the two of you make decisions that might have been bad for her? Probably. But you aren't responsible for her death. The police cleared you, and you let everyone in town think you had hurt her."

"I did. I hurt Allison badly." Dante blinked the tears out of his eyes and slowly stood up a little straighter. "I have to live with that for the rest of my life. I was selfish and did what my father wanted, and it ultimately cost Allison her life. I can never change that, no matter how much I might want to."

Beau took Dante's hand, drawing him out of the hallway and slowly through the rooms to the kitchen. He'd seen the shadows of this in Dante's behavior and knew there had been something very traumatic in his past. As a substance-abuse counselor, he knew the signs of families of addicts, but he also knew that the families of those with mental illness went through many of the same challenges. And God knew Dante had been through a lot, compounded by guilt—piles of guilt.

"Come on. I need you to finish up the salad so I can make the rest of dinner." Beau turned on the heat under the water and got the pasta going once again, then cut up the chicken into bite-sized pieces.

"What do I do now?" Dante asked. "I don't feel any different."

"Unlike in the movies or on television, you don't have some sort of epiphany and then the sun comes out and all is right with the world. It doesn't happen like that. You confided what happened, and I can tell you that she took her own life."

"I know that. I've always known that. But it doesn't mean I'm...." Dante huffed and finished with the lettuce, transferring it to a bowl. Beau pulled out the croutons and handed Dante a tomato and a small onion. "These don't go in Caesar."

"I like them. Cut the onion up really fine, and the tomato is firm enough for small pieces. It adds a little something other than lettuce to the salad. I have some cheese too, and I brought some of my homemade dressing." Beau pulled the jar out of the bag. "We don't need to dress it until we're ready to eat, though."

Dante went back to work while Beau put the pasta in to cook. "Her family doesn't know…," Dante said.

Beau stirred the pasta and lifted his gaze. "Doesn't know what?" he asked, a little confused.

"That she took her own life. I doubt she planned it, but her family believes that suicide is a fast trip to hell, so they think it was an accident, which they still blame me for. I can live with that as long as they accept that Allison is at peace now. At least I hope she is." Dante wiped his eyes with the back of his hand.

Beau wanted to help Dante so badly, but years of guilt weren't going to be erased in a matter of hours. But the way Dante took responsibility and sheltered Allison's family through this made Beau love him even more. Dante was willing to take whatever the town and even Allison's family thought of him in order to protect Allison's memory. That kind of man needed to be treasured, not vilified.

Beau made up the pesto sauce with his own basil pesto, a little cream, and some pine nuts for crunch. Then he drained the pasta, sauced it, added the chicken, and stirred it all together. "Go ahead and mix everything in the bowl and add some of the Caesar dressing. Not too much—we can always add some more." Beau finished up his dish and watched Dante. Then he found some plates and bowls and dished everything up before heading to the table near the window.

"I never eat in here."

"It's nice, and that dining room is fine for a dinner party of twelve, but not for just the two of us." He set down the plates and found some cutlery. Then he went in search of glasses before checking out the refrigerator. Wine wasn't something either of them needed at the moment, but he found a pitcher of iced tea and poured two large glasses before bringing them to the table.

"This is great," Dante said around a mouthful of pasta. "You'll have to tell Harriet how you made it."

"I bet she already knows what to do. This isn't all that special. If you ask her for it, I'm sure she'll make it for you any time." Beau reached across the table to take Dante's hand. "You need to relax."

"I keep thinking about Allison."

Beau blew out his breath between his teeth. "Guilt is a useless emotion. It changes nothing and keeps us locked in the past. You have to let it go."

"I don't know how." Dante took another bite, and Beau wished he could take away the pain Dante carried with him, but he wasn't a miracle worker. "I try not to think about it all the time."

"Letting go isn't forgetting what happened. It's letting yourself realize that you weren't responsible for Allison's death. Sometimes a cigar is just a cigar, and an accident is an accident. Life is such that someone isn't responsible for everything. Sometimes shit happens."

Dante rolled his eyes. "You're just full of platitudes tonight, aren't you?"

Beau swallowed a bite of salad. "It made you smile."

Dante shook his head. "Bastard."

"Come on. You don't want to be miserable—I can tell. You want to let this go, but you've been hanging on to this guilt for so long, it's become a part of you. But guilt and pain aren't who you are. You also aren't this Beast persona that others have labeled you with."

"Then who am I?" Dante asked the question with all seriousness.

"You're who you want to be. Your dad tried to foist his vision of you as his son off on the world and superimpose it on you. It's what he did, and you allowed him to do it. Your dad is gone, and now you need to decide who you are. Not who the town thinks you are, or Allison's family… anyone."

Dante sighed. "Shit, you never have easy questions with quick answers, do you?"

"Nope." Beau took another bite of pasta. "But seeing yourself through the hard questions to the difficult answers usually ends in a meaningful result. Easy questions with quick answers are forgotten just as fast." He continued eating. "Don't expect things to change overnight, and I hate to say it, but they might not change at all. I don't know. But you've told me what happened...."

"Yes...?"

"You notice that I didn't run away or call you a Beast or any other names." Beau lifted his eyebrows as he held his fork above his plate.

"But maybe you should have. What if...?"

Beau chuckled. "What are you afraid is going to happen?"

"I don't know," Dante confessed.

Hearing that tone was disconcerting. Beau would much rather have Dante growl and storm through the kitchen. This resigned and almost cowed Dante wasn't the man he'd come to know or wanted to see. Part of what attracted him to Dante was his strength and the way he held his head high in the face of everyone else's derision. Dante had a backbone of steel, and Beau hated to see him like this.

"Then deal with what happens when it comes." Beau returned to his dinner, eating slowly, watching Dante as he seemed to process what Beau was trying to tell him. It wasn't long before all the pasta and salad were gone. The events of the evening hadn't dulled Dante's appetite, which Beau took as a good thing.

"What do you want to do now?"

"I need to clean up so Harriet doesn't lock me out of the kitchen." Beau squeezed Dante's hand. "I like this kitchen. It's a dream to work in." He smiled, and eventually Dante did the same. Beau wasn't under the illusion that the years of guilt and shame were gone, but he hoped he'd been able to lighten Dante's burden somewhat. "I'll get the fruit, and we can take it in and watch a movie or something." He didn't think jumping into bed was a good idea at the moment. His body was keen on the idea, but his head told him to take it slow. Dante had been through a great deal by reliving what happened with Allison.

Dante stood, took the plates, and set them on the counter. He opened the door of the dishwasher, staring inside. "I have to confess, I don't really know what to do."

Beau chuckled and cleared the rest of the dishes. He pulled out the racks and loaded the plates inside. "It's not that hard."

"But which buttons do you press to start it?" Dante stared at the various settings once Beau closed the door.

"I think we can leave that for Harriet. She'll know it best." Beau opened the refrigerator door, pulled out the berries he'd cleaned, and then followed Dante out of the kitchen and through to a small room off Dante's office where he had a television. "This house is so huge."

"I know. I swear there are places I've yet to discover." Dante settled on the comfortable older dark plaid sofa, and Beau sat next to him.

"Are you all right?" Beau scooted closer so Dante could wrap his arms around him. He liked the security of Dante's embrace. How could people think the things of him that they did? If only they could get to know him, none of that would be possible.

"Yes, I think so. Nothing I can do to help Allison now." Dante breathed gently into Beau's ear. It wasn't sexy, just gentle.

"You still care for her and remember the friendship and the good things you had."

"Of course."

"Then that's all you can do. You protected her family from what would hurt them even more than losing their daughter. None of us will ever know if Allison meant to hurt herself or not."

"I like to think it was an accident. I don't really know. She was so angry at me and herself that night. I think things had gone too far for her, and...." Dante swallowed. "She said she wanted to have a baby, and I almost took her to bed, because I wanted one too. I probably could have closed my eyes or something... and given her what she said she wanted...." Dante tugged him closer, shaking slightly.

"That wouldn't have changed anything. You have to know that. Things with Allison, for herself, were getting out of control. Only medical help would do any good, and if she was fighting it, there are limited things that you could have done. People have to want and be willing to accept help before anything meaningful can happen. I know you blame yourself for all of this, but Allison has to shoulder a lot of the blame herself." Beau met his gaze.

"What makes you say that?"

"Allison agreed to marry you. Why? She knew you were gay, and then, after some time, she's trying to change the arrangement, wanting children, things she had to know weren't going to happen. Why?" Beau leaned back so Dante could see him plainly. "What was Allison hoping to get?"

"Security?" Dante answered. "A better life?"

"You really don't know, do you?"

Dante shook his head. "She wasn't dating at the time, and she and I had been spending a lot of time together."

"Do you think she was in love with you?" Beau asked. Dante gasped, stilled, and remained quiet for far longer than Beau expected. "Do you think she fell in love with you before your marriage, and she accepted because she thought that over time you'd grow to love her the way she loved you?"

Dante nodded. "It makes sense now. She... I remember the way she used to look at me when she was unguarded. I didn't think about it then, but I remember those looks. It was as though she were longing for something, wishing.... How could I have been so stupid?" He pulled Beau to him, burying his face against his shoulder. Dante was crying... and the Beast was dead. At least Beau hoped so.

CHAPTER 7

DANTE WOKE in the middle of the night, alone. Sometimes jet lag really stunk, like when he wanted to sleep and woke up at strange hours. He and Beau had watched a movie and then gone to bed. Thankfully, Beau never mentioned the way he'd nearly lost it. The wave of hurt that had overtaken him had easily crested his defenses and he hadn't been able to hold it in. Beau had sat with him, silent, and once it passed, they watched Mel Brooks' *The Producers*, the original movie. It felt good to laugh, even if his eyes still held the last vestiges of tears. Laughter was something that had been absent from his life for a long time.

He listened for any indication that Beau was in the bathroom, but heard nothing. Beau's side of the bed was cool, so he'd left some time earlier. Dante felt a growl rising in his throat. Had Beau left him after all? Dante had spent years convincing himself that he didn't need anyone, had finally let down his guard, and now Beau was gone. Dante hated the thought that he'd been left alone once more.

A creak from outside the door caught his attention. Dante pushed back the covers, turning on the soft light next to the bed. He yanked on his robe and pulled the door open the rest of the way. A sliver of light from Allison's room led him there. That room had been closed up since her death. No one went in, except maybe the housekeeper a few times a year. He hadn't been in there since her death. He had simply closed it up and left it that way.

"What are you doing?" Dante barked more loudly than he intended.

Beau squeaked from where he knelt near the side of the bed. "I was curious and couldn't sleep." He got to his feet, his robe partially open.

For a second Dante forgot his anger, enthralled by the wide slice of visible golden skin. He shook his head to clear it. "So you decided to rummage through Allison's things?" He put his hands on his hips, glaring at Beau before his gaze drifted to the bathroom door, where the light was also on. "Is this how you usually behave?" His hands balled into fists before he could stop them.

"Dante," Beau said gently but without remorse. There was steel underlying the softness. "You told me what happened, but I wanted to see if there was anything that Allison could tell us."

Dante narrowed his eyes. "What the fuck are you talking about?"

"This is her room, right?" Beau sounded so fucking logical, and Dante's heart raced with aggression and anger.

"Of course it is."

"And from the look of things, no one has been in here since she died? It certainly doesn't look like anyone has been in here."

Dante took a look at the thick coat of dust and realized his assumption was wrong. Even the housekeepers Roberts employed had left the room alone. Cobwebs hung from the ceiling down to the tops of the heavy velvet curtains, which had been drawn closed. He could tell what Beau had touched simply by the marks in the dust. "No. I closed the room after she died and didn't come in here. What does that have to do with you snooping through the house?"

Beau walked over to him. "This is where Allison would keep her things, and anything private, maybe containing her thoughts, would be in here. Sometimes mentally ill people believe they're the ones who are sane and everyone else is wrong. To help prove it, they sometimes write things down. I've helped people who have filled dozens of notebooks. I was hoping to find something that would help explain to you what Allison was thinking and maybe give you some peace."

And just like that, Dante's anger faded. Fuck it all, Beau had been trying to help him. "Huh…."

Beau placed his hands on Dante's shoulders. "You're so used to everyone seeing the bad side of you and being on your own that you don't believe anyone would want to help you." Beau's huge, beautiful eyes cut right through Dante's aggression, and it melted away like snow in July. He lowered his gaze, and Beau touched his chin. "Never forget that I see you for who you are. I have never seen the Beast. I've always seen Dante, and it's time the rest of the world and this crazy town does the same."

"It is?" Dante managed those few words before his mouth went dry. How could he argue with Beau when he was the object of such intensity? He'd been angry, and in those seconds, Beau had looked at him as though he were some sort of god that Beau wanted to eat for lunch, in the hottest way possible. Dante had thought that he had things together, that he knew his place in life, and that he could be content with that. He'd never been so wrong in his life. There was no way in hell he could live without this man standing in front of him.

"Yes. You are not a beast." Beau walked to the bathroom door and turned out the light. Then he switched off the one next to the bed, plunging the room into near total darkness. Taking Dante's hand, he led him back to his bedroom.

"I'm not?" Dante asked as they walked.

"No. You're a person, just like anyone else, and this… our lives aren't a fairy tale." Beau chuckled. "Besides, if you're the Beast, well… we both sure as hell know that I'm no Beauty."

Dante disagreed vehemently with what Beau had just said. He closed the bedroom door once they were inside, went to the corner of the room, and spun the cheval mirror so it faced them. "Come here." He tugged Beau in front of him, turning him toward the mirror, and slipped the robe off his shoulders.

"I told you," Beau whispered as they both looked at his reflection. "The scars make me look… well, you see them. You know

I'll never be anyone's Beauty." Beau turned and undid the knot in the belt of Dante's robe, sliding it off his shoulders. "Sometimes I wish you could see what I do." He stepped to the side. "You're the one who's beautiful." He ran his fingers lightly down Dante's chest, creating a trail of fire in their wake.

Dante rotated Beau around, pressed his chest to Beau's back, his cock sliding along his perfect butt, and wrapped his arms around Beau's waist. He kissed Beau's neck, then lifted his gaze to the mirror. In the low light, Beau's golden skin glowed and the scars faded before his eyes. "You are a beauty. It glows from inside you. I can see that—I think maybe I always have." Dante didn't turn away, blinking as all he saw was the most incredible man he had ever met. There were no scars, only gentleness and caring. "It's what's on the inside that counts." Dante held Beau closer, heat building from deep inside, bursting out wherever Beau touched him.

"What are you saying?" Beau asked.

"I may be a beast, but I'm your Beast, just like you're my Beauty. The other half of me." Dante had never felt as content or quite as complete before.

Beau turned just enough to catch Dante's lips. Dante skimmed his fingers gently over Beau's delicate throat, then cupped his jaw as he kissed him deeper. Dante ran his tongue over the seam of Beau's lips, not able to get enough of him.

"How about you endeavor to be only my Beast and no one else's, then?" Beau said. "Let everyone else see the man you truly are, and you be my Beast in bed. Because that's where I like him best." Beau ground his butt into him, and Dante tried like hell to stifle a deep growl, failing miserably.

Beau laughed, and Dante turned him around and hoisted him into his arms, stalking toward the bed. "You're being a fucking tease."

"I am not," Beau argued. "I fully intend to put out, but not before I drive the beast inside you crazy." He grinned evilly.

"You already have." Dante set Beau on the bed with a bounce and stalked onto the mattress, coming to the end of his patience.

He kissed him as his hands roamed over Beau's golden skin. He wanted all of him at the same time, his entire body thrumming with each beat of his heart, control already slipping away. Beau held him, his own fingers exploring, and when Beau lightly pinched a nipple, Dante reared up, hissing in exquisite delight. Beau followed him, sucking the lightly abused nipple between his lips, teasing him until Dante could hardly see straight. "You're playing with fire."

"No, I think that's you." Beau grinned up at him, and Dante cupped his cheeks, holding him still so he could feast on Beau's full, already swollen lips. He knew Beau was right. Beau was pure fire, and Dante would play with him for the rest of his life if Beau would have him.

"Damn," Dante breathed. He could feel the heat and wanted even more. He tugged Beau to him, pressing their bodies together, hips rocking slowly on their own, instinct taking over.

Beau stretched, and Dante heard the drawer beside the bed slide open. "You have to have some of the damn things, and...." He groaned and pressed a condom packet into his hand. "That's what I want."

Dante's head spun a minute. Beau gazed at him, all heat and need, sending Dante into flight. He hadn't thought anyone could ever want him. He'd only thought that he was broken and that his chances at happiness had been used up or thrown away, and here Beau was, offering him something he'd never even hoped to get.

"Are you sure I'm good enough?" Dante had to know if this was real.

"I knew that night I first saw you at the benefit." Beau wrapped his arms around his neck, drawing him downward, but Dante held still.

"How could you?" Dante asked, his lips inches from Beau's, looking for something deep in Beau's eyes.

"I don't know. I just did. You were the infamous Dante Bartholomew, and you could have spoken to anyone in the room, but you spent most of your time with Bobby and then me. I saw your pain, and…." Beau paused. "Then you looked at me and the pain receded. There was happiness in its place. Not for long, but it was there. The real Dante lay under all that pain and guilt, and whether you meant to or not, you let me see him."

Dante swallowed as the last of the walls around his heart crashed to rubble. The roar of their collapse sounded in his ears—or maybe that was the beating of his heart coming alive again after so long. Dante wasn't sure which it was. Maybe it was both.

"Make love to me," Beau said softly, but he could have shouted it from the rooftops. The effect on Dante was instant.

"Why don't you make love to me?" Dante asked as he swallowed hard.

Beau stilled under him, brushing his hand over Dante's forehead, looking deep into his eyes. "Because you're about to freak out any second. And that's not what I like." Beau kissed him, sending another wave of fire rushing through Dante. "I want you to be happy, and you being in charge, driving me full force to the moon and back, is exactly what I want."

"But I don't want to be selfish, and…." His head spun again. Dante had never offered himself in that way to anyone, and he'd done it because he wanted to show Beau how much he cared and how important Beau was to him. It shocked Dante that Beau could read him so well already to know that wasn't really part of him.

Beau grinned. "Fucking me from here to eternity isn't being selfish—it's giving of yourself… over and over again. So let's get with the giving, because I sure as hell need it. You promised me the Beast, and I want him."

Dante growled, and Beau tightened his legs around Dante's waist, inflaming him, leaving Dante no doubt that what he'd said was the truth.

"I asked before and I'll say it again. Make love to me, Dante." Beau's eyes had shifted to the deepest blue, and they drew him in. Dante brushed his forehead, leaning even closer, half afraid he'd tumble into those huge eyes and never come out again. He closed the final distance between them, kissing Beau as he arched under him.

Breathless, Dante saw spots when he pulled away once again. He fished for the packet he'd dropped on the bedding and found it without too much difficulty. Dante ripped it open and prepared himself and then Beau before taking his position once again. This time when he kissed Beau, he gasped against his lips as Beau's pressure and heat surrounded him.

Beau sucked on Dante's lip, holding him tighter, shuddering slightly as they slowly joined more completely. Dante didn't want to hurt Beau at all. This was about joy and happiness, things that had been missing from his life for a long time.

"You are my Beauty," Dante whispered as Beau gripped his entire length.

"So full," Beau groaned, then slowly rocked back and forth. It was just enough for Dante to understand Beau's preferred pace, and he picked up his timing, holding Beau closely to him. Dante listened for the hitches in Beau's breath. They told him when he'd touched Beau just right, and when the breaths became shallow, Dante knew he was driving Beau toward his release. He wanted to hear it, see it, even smell the tang of it.

"That's it. Show me what I do to you." Dante gasped as energy built inside him to the point of near bursting. He watched and listened to Beau, determined to hold off.

"What are you whispering?" Beau asked as he took Dante deep.

"Unsexy things so I don't come too soon," Dante admitted. He needed to keep his control for a little while longer, and that seemed to be doing the trick. Of course, Beau's laughter had the same effect, until it shifted to soft moans of delight. Dante cut off those sounds with his lips on Beau's, drinking in the sweetness and passion. He was so incredible. Dante adored every inch of him. He ran his hands along Beau's chest, the now familiar lines and bumps only adding to his pleasure because they were uniquely Beau, his Beau… his Beauty.

Beau was the only person who had tried to look beneath the walls he'd put up. Somehow Beau had seen to the heart of him when Dante hadn't even known what was there. He loved him, and Beau needed to know it. So Dante showed him in the way he knew how. When Dante threw his head back, squeezing his eyes closed because he was so close, Beau cried out, shuddering beneath him, clamping hard onto Dante's cock, his release spilling between them.

He sent Dante over the edge in seconds, ears ringing, flashes behind his eyes. Dante had always thought that the whole fireworks thing during sex was some sort of metaphor, but it was real. Small points of light danced across his vision. Dante stilled and let the warmth and tingling of release wash over him.

Beau pulled him close, and Dante's arms gave out. He held Beau tight, shuddering slightly through the effects of afterglow. This was where he was supposed to be. This felt right. For the first time in his life, this was perfection for him.

Beau ran his thumbs under Dante's eyes. "There's no need for tears. This is a happy time."

Dante nodded, leaving his eyes closed. He rarely cried. In his whole life, he could count on one hand the number of times he'd cried for anything. Hell, even after Allison's death, when his life and the decisions he'd made closed around him, he hadn't cried. "I don't understand why."

"Maybe it's for the times when they wouldn't come." Beau wrapped his arms around him, and Dante rested on top of him, Beau's heat reaching bone-deep, soul-deep, warming Dante in a way he never thought possible. "It's all right."

"I did love Allison in a way, but not at all like I love you." Dante clutched Beau and let that realization wash over him like rain. He was in love. This was what true love felt like.

"I love you too, Beast and all…," Beau told him, and they shared another kiss that Dante felt to the depths of his soul.

When he woke again, Dante was alone once more.

Beau sat in the chair at the foot of the bed, reading. "Finally. I didn't want to wake you up." He put the book aside and stretched his arms over his head. Then he stood and stalked over to the bed like a cat eyeing its prey. Beau's robe fell open and he slithered out of it, letting the dark blue fabric fall to the floor.

Music played from somewhere in the pile of clothing on the other chair, and Beau huffed for a second before continuing toward the bed. "It can go to voicemail. You're more important." Beau leaped and Dante caught him. They laughed together as heat built instantly between them. The phone rang again, and Beau groaned, then huffed as he climbed off the bed. "This had better be really good." He searched through the clothes, his butt wagging a little as he bent over.

Dante sat up, enjoying the view as Beau found his phone and silenced the infernal ringing. He hated that ringtone, which sounded like the blaring phone from his childhood.

"Angie? What's going on?" Beau said, sounding so chipper, and turned. They shared a brief smile, and then Dante watched as it slipped from Beau's face. His eyes clouded and his mouth opened in surprise and near horror.

Dante pushed back the covers, got out of the bed, and hurried to him. In the few seconds it took to reach him, Beau had turned completely pale.

"Is anyone inside?" He shivered, and Dante took him in his arms. He wasn't sure what was going on, but whatever it was had scared Beau to his core. "I'll be right there." Beau clutched his phone as he leaned on Dante. "Yeah. Do whatever you need, though word is going to spread quickly. Help them as best you can. I'm on my way." Beau hung up and met Dante's gaze. "The Center is on fire."

Dante kept his thoughts clear. "Okay. You get dressed." He set Beau on the chair and pulled open the bedroom door. "Roberts!" He closed the door and yanked clothes out of his dresser.

A soft knock announced their reinforcements. "Sir."

Dante glanced at Beau, who had his pants on. "Come in." Dante stepped into a pair of jeans as the door opened. "I need the car around front right away. If Juan isn't available, then you'll need to do it. The Community Center is on fire, and Beau and I need to get down there." He turned away and pulled his shirt on. Dante never heard the door close or anything other than Beau's groan of despair.

"It's gone."

"Finish dressing and we'll be on our way." Dante pressed some clean socks into Beau's hand and sat on the edge of the bed. He was dressed and ready, helping Beau, who seemed in shock. When he was clothed, Dante guided him down the stairs and right out the front door to the limousine. Roberts was behind the wheel as they climbed in, and as soon as the door shut, they took off at a speed faster than Dante thought possible in the land yacht.

They could only get so close before they were stopped by barricades. Beau got out, and Dante hurried to follow him.

"Sir. I'm sorry, but you can't get any closer," a uniformed officer told them.

Dante stepped forward. "He's the director of the Center, and you sure as hell know who I am." He actually growled, and the officer blinked. "Now, let us through." He allowed his tone to make the threat that there would be hell to pay, and the officer stood aside. Dante put an arm around Beau to help ensure he stayed upright, and they approached where Angie stood with a small group of others.

As soon as Angie saw Beau, she pulled him into a hug, and the two of them stood together, crying against each other's shoulder. Dante turned and saw Mayor Grant standing a few paces away, watching. Dante looked at the building just as the roof collapsed, sending a flare of sparks and smoke into the air.

"Tragic."

Somehow Dante wasn't convinced by the mayor's tone, given his eagerness to sell the property. "I'm sure you think so. Looks like you'll get your way."

"I'm not happy about this!" Mayor Grant snapped, losing his usual politician's smarmy cool.

"Your Honor," the fire captain said as he approached. Beau moved to stand next to him, and Dante automatically put his arm around him.

"Peter, what's going on?" Dante asked. He wasn't going to wait while Mayor Grant played politics. He didn't have the patience.

"Mr. Bartholomew."

"This is Beau Clarity, the Center's director. What can you tell us?"

Peter turned to Beau. "Was anything stored in the building? Particularly anything flammable?"

"God, no. There were things in the basement when I took over, but those were cleaned out. We're a health facility, and we help children as well as adults. I didn't want anything that could be a danger in the building. Why?"

"We turned off the gas service as soon as we arrived. We were told that no one was inside, so after confirming, we wet the fire from the outside. Five minutes later something exploded, sending a rush through the center of the building. I was hoping you could tell us what that might be."

"Nothing that we kept inside. The most explosive thing in there would be Angie's coffee. There was nothing flammable, and the only chemicals we had were a few cleaning supplies. And I only got organic, water-based cleaners because some of our kids have allergies. Since we helped people with substance-abuse issues, there was nothing inside that would tempt any of them at all. Nothing alcohol- or ether-based. Not even a bottle of cough syrup. Nothing," Beau said, adamant. "It was a 100 percent safe environment in that regard."

Peter nodded and made some notes. "I thought the fire was behaving suspiciously, but that helps confirm it."

"You mean it was deliberate," Dante said for clarification.

"It looks that way. An empty building, even one of this age, will burn, but the fire will spread in an almost predictable way and time. This fire spread fast and hot. It was fueled most likely by an accelerant." Peter turned as a hiss went up from the building and the flames began to die. Streams of water made paths into the now-hollow shell.

Dante turned to Mayor Grant. "Know anything that could help?"

Mayor Grant looked at Beau. "My office and the council members have been getting letters and calls from numerous citizens for days. Dozens of people have stopped me on the street to tell me what your Center has done for them." He definitely appeared sheepish. "I don't think the sale was going to be approved."

"Was anyone specifically notified of this change in enthusiasm?" Dante asked, already beginning to understand what the answer was going to be. "Did you notify anyone?" He let the authority ring in his voice.

"I might have told Bledsoe that he needed to back off. At least for a while."

What a slimy piece of crap. Withdraw the offer now and live to fight another day when the climate might have changed. It's what Dante might have done if the shoe were on the other foot. Still, it was a shitty thing to do with a town asset that was being used for the benefit of the community.

"And now, with this…." Dante motioned to the still-burning ruin. "What do you think the council will do?" He raised his eyebrows.

Mayor Grant blanched. "If they decide to rebuild with the insurance money, then the Center will get a whole new facility." He glanced at Beau.

"He was with me all night, so don't even go there." Dante stepped closer. "You may have made yourself a party to arson, Mayor.

I suggest you think on that very carefully and take the appropriate action before the good citizens of this town decide to take it for you. The sale Harper wanted was going to fall through, you told him so, and now the building goes up in flames. It doesn't take a huge leap of faith to see who might be the one to gain from it."

"I had no idea he'd set fire to the place… or if he even did."

"Maybe, but I will be speaking to the police so they can investigate." Dante glared at him. "Just to be clear, the state police will be called." The mayor and the police chief were too close, in Dante's opinion. "Now, I suggest you go on home and mull over whatever future you think you might have." It was time the town had new leadership anyway. Fresh ideas were needed, and Mayor Grant was about as far from anything fresh and new as it was possible to get.

Dante turned away and found Beau still watching the Center burn.

"What are we going to do?"

"Find temporary facilities. No one was hurt, and it was just a building. The important components of the Center, the people, are still here and available. But right now, we need to get you back home. There isn't anything either you or Angie can do. The police and fire officials need to do their jobs." Dante turned Beau away from the building and back to where Angie had wandered.

"Well…?" she asked.

"No matter what we were hoping for, we'll have to find temporary housing for the Center now. The kids and everyone we help are going to be so upset." Beau clung to Dante. "I had such plans."

"They can still come to pass."

Beau shook his head. "Are you kidding? Most organizations fold over something like this. Insurance doesn't cover all the costs of rebuilding, and the town is going to get the money, not us. We'll get some for our contents, but that's it. Then the board needs to allocate the money for the Center, and it's too easy to send it somewhere else. So basically the Center ends up in the waste bin because the money is too good not to mess with." Beau slumped his shoulders, sounding defeated. "It's hard enough to get or keep a program like ours running, let alone make it come back from a loss of the building. That's why I was fighting so hard to stay where we were." He shivered, and Dante gently guided him back toward where Roberts had parked the car.

A crash rumbled from behind them, and Dante shielded Beau automatically as the outer front wall of the building collapsed inward, bringing the rest of the outer shell down on the interior. Beau took it like a blow.

"Angie, do you need a ride or anything?" Dante asked, but she shook her head, not looking away from the smoldering ruin.

"I'll be fine." She didn't move, and Beau hurried to Angie and carefully tugged her over to the car.

"She lives just a block away."

Both of them looked heartbroken. Dante opened the car door and let Beau guide Angie inside. Then he got in as well, and Roberts glided away from the scene. Dante had never been so eager to leave something behind as he was the scene of that fire. Angie and Beau hung on to each other, and Dante hated to admit that he was jealous. He wanted Beau's attention.

"It'll be all right. We'll figure things out," Beau told her with no conviction behind his words. He gave Roberts directions, and when they pulled up in front of Angie's small house, Dante let her out. She half trudged up the walk and into the house like her world had come crashing down along with those brick walls.

Beau settled next to him, curling on the seat, and Dante gathered him close. "What do you want me to do?" Dante asked. "I can make sure you have the finances and the location to rebuild. You know that. I can put pressure on the council to make sure they don't touch a cent of the insurance money and only use it to rebuild. I can make my own donation to start the ball rolling." He stroked Beau's soft hair. "What do you want?" He had never cared so much about what someone else wanted in his life as he did right at that moment.

"I want to find out who did this and make them pay. Those kids…. They're going to be heartbroken." Beau stayed still, and Dante knew it wasn't the kids who were hurting, but the man in his arms. Beau lifted his head. "It was that Bledsoe guy, wasn't it? Allison's brother? He wasn't going to get the property as it was and wanted to tear the building down anyway, so now he gets what he wanted."

"We don't know that or have any proof."

"Then get it. You asked what I want. Get me that. Find out who hated us so much that they burned down a mental health center." Tears glistened in Beau's eyes, and Dante pulled him closer. There were some things in his control, but getting people to confess to a crime wasn't in his wheelhouse. He knew that, and so did Beau. This was the grief and anger of loss, and Dante held him as Beau fell quiet. "I'm sorry."

"We will figure things out." Dante had no doubt they would, but right now he needed to get Beau back to the house. The professionals needed to do their jobs, and then Dante would get some of his people on the problem of helping Beau figure out a temporary location for the Center.

The car glided into the drive and then up to the house. Dante got out of the car and helped Beau inside and down to the kitchen.

"I heard what happened," Harriet said, opening the refrigerator and pulling things out. From the looks of things, she was getting ready to feed an army, but within minutes she had the entire kitchen smelling of onions and peppers, then placed a plate with one of her fluffy omelets in front of each of them.

Harriet could be described as a rather tiny woman in her early forties, but she was a force to be reckoned with. She also had a heart of gold and showed love with food. It was one of the things that had helped him get through the loss of Allison.

"Thank you." Beau shared a smile with her, and she patted his shoulder.

"You're a sweetheart." She turned to Dante. "Don't let this one get away."

Dante smiled. "You like him because he used your kitchen and didn't make a mess."

"Unlike some people I could name," Harriet groused, though Dante knew it was an act.

"Is he really that bad?" Beau asked.

Harriet scowled. "Did he tell you about the cookies?"

Beau nodded.

"That man is a menace in the kitchen. He could burn water." Her lips softened to a gentle smile. "Don't tell him, but he's the best employer I've ever had. I just don't want him to get a big head." Harriet winked at him and went back to work.

"What are you making?" Dante asked as she pulled out a large bowl and a container of flour.

"Cookies. I figure you'll need them later. I'll bring some to you once they're finished."

Dante was grateful, and he ate his omelet quietly, watching as Beau picked at his, eating a little, his lips narrow with worry.

"I'm sorry for being… I don't know…."

The wind had been knocked out of his sails, and Dante would give anything to have them full again. He knew it was too soon, and Beau needed a chance to grieve and try to figure out what he was going to do.

Dante finished eating, and once Beau was done, they thanked Harriet and Dante carefully led Beau to the sitting room.

"I'm going to make some calls. Is that okay? If you need me, I'll be in my office." He turned on the television and made sure Beau was comfortable, then went into the office and picked up the phone. "Yates," Dante said as soon as he answered.

"Dante, what can I do for you?"

"I need you to get in touch with the Foundation board. We need to find a new location for the Community Center. The building burned down this morning. The authorities believe the fire was set on purpose. They're looking into it, but the staff will need temporary facilities. See what you can come up with. Their old building was about five thousand square feet or so. Mostly it was activity rooms, as well as smaller spaces for counseling sessions and things like that. It doesn't have to be perfect because it will be temporary."

"And the cost…?"

"Get the Foundation to approve it." Dante wasn't going to argue about it. "Our mission is to help the community, and this is a lot more important than some beautification project." The mayor's comment still stuck in his craw.

"This wouldn't happen to have anything to do with a certain blue-eyed man who runs the Center, does it?" Yates sounded amused, and Dante growled deep in his throat. "Sorry. But I had to ask."

"Why? Beau is a dear man, and he doesn't deserve to be the subject of rumor and speculation." They could say what they wanted about him, but no one was going to disparage Beau.

Yates cleared his throat. "I'll get right on it."

"Good. And contact the state police while you're at it. Ask them to send someone here to look into the fire and what's going on. The mayor had his hand in this deal to sell the building that housed the Center, and I'm not sure that he and the police chief are capable of keeping their personal agendas out of any investigation." Dante was willing to use his connections to make sure the people in authority behaved the way they should.

"You got it."

"Thanks." Dante ended the call and looked to the door, where Beau leaned on the frame, then came inside.

"You don't quit, do you?" he said, sounding angry.

Dante stood and walked to him. "No. I'm a man of action. My lawyer is looking into potential temporary locations for you. Once he has something, you can see if they'll fit your basic needs. I know they won't be perfect, but we'll get the Center up and running again." He enfolded Beau into his arms. "I know this has been a shitty day, but we'll figure it out and get through it." He had to try to make things better for Beau. He held him tight, and after a few seconds, Beau looked up at him, smiling.

"I always knew this man was inside you."

"I thought you might be angry with me," Dante whispered. Sometimes he had to admit that his instincts with others were crap.

"Why would I be?" Beau snuggled against him, his voice muffled against Dante's shirt.

"Because you didn't want me stepping in before."

Beau lifted his face and rolled his eyes dramatically. "That was when we were trying to save the Center and show the board that it had community support. It needed the community behind it—it still does—but now it's going to need a champion, and I can see that's what it has in you… in us."

"It does." Though Dante had to admit that if Beau had asked him to champion the cause of feeding blind lab rats, he'd do it as long as it made Beau happy. "What else do we need to do?"

"I don't know. I need to call some of our volunteers and let them know what's going on." Beau's phone rang, and he pulled it out of his pocket.

"You have to get a different ringtone. That one drives me crazy," Dante said of the loud, jarring, old-fashioned telephone ring. "Maybe harps or something." After all, Beau was angelic in Dante's eyes. He turned away, wondering when he'd become such a sap. Not that he cared in the least. He was a sap in love, and that was all that mattered.

Beau nodded and answered the call. Dante provided him the courtesy of not listening in as he answered questions from one of his people. He didn't know anything right now, but Dante loved how gentle he was with them, even after call after call, answering what had to be the same questions again and again. Dante continued working; just being in the same room with Beau was good enough.

When his phone rang, he answered it quietly.

"Mr. Bartholomew?" a rather official-sounding voice said.

"Yes."

"I'm Officer Howard with the Maryland State Police. I received word to call you."

"Thank you," Dante said, then explained what had happened. "I know this is unusual, but the mayor, and by extension the police chief, are too close to this with their own agendas. All I'm asking is that someone watch them so they follow the rules and do their jobs. Besides, we don't have the fire investigative tools available to us that your department does."

"You really believe this fire was arson?" Officer Howard asked.

"The fire captain thought so because of the explosion and how quickly the building burned. He thought an accelerant was at play. But we're a small town without the resources and expertise of larger cities. I'd appreciate your help."

"That isn't a problem. I'm stationed in St. George, and I'll be able to come over and have a look around to see if I can provide any assistance."

"If you have questions for me or the director of the facility, you can reach either of us at this number." He wasn't going to hide the fact that he and Beau were involved. "At the moment Beau has been on the phone to his volunteers and some of the people he serves to try to reassure them. We are already working to find a temporary location."

"All right. I'll look into what I can find and see if there is anything we can do to help." It was a standard answer, but Dante felt better that the chief of police, who reported to the mayor, would feel some pressure to do what was right rather than what was politically expedient for his boss.

"Thank you." Dante ended the call, wondering what else he could do to help. His phone rang again, this time from the porcelain works, and he spent the next few hours on the phone taking care of normal business. By the time he was through, Dante was hungry. Beau had spent just as much time on the phone and looked exhausted.

Roberts came in with a light lunch, and they ate between additional phone calls.

Near the end of the day, Roberts knocked on the office door. "Sir, there's someone here for you. It's a police officer."

"Thank you." Dante stood and went to meet him, with Beau right behind him. Judging by the uniform and then the name emblazoned on his chest, this was Officer Howard. "I'm Dante Bartholomew, and this is Beau Clarity. Thank you for agreeing to help us."

"You're welcome." Officer Howard took off his hat, and Dante motioned toward the office. "Thank you."

"Would you like anything?" Roberts asked as they entered. "Coffee perhaps?"

"That would be nice, Roberts. Thank you," Dante answered, anxious to find out what Officer Howard had for them.

Officer Howard didn't waste any time. After sitting, he opened his notebook and said, "An hour ago we issued and executed an arrest warrant."

"Harper Bledsoe?" Dante asked.

"Yes. He didn't set fire to the building himself. He paid some indigent people to do it. I think he expected that, once they got inside, they'd be caught in the fire. As near as we could tell, all of the doors were locked." Officer Howard paused when Roberts brought in a tray and then began again once he left the room. "The two men were very drunk when we caught up to them. They were able to identify Bledsoe and explained that he paid them in a case of liquor, which they immediately began consuming, at first for Dutch courage and then because of what they'd done."

"Why would he do that?"

"It's what we're hoping to get from him. But our theory is that he got them inside and then locked them in the building. His plan was that they wouldn't get out, and no one would question or miss them once the fire had killed them. The two men discovered the locked doors and climbed out one of the back windows before hitting their stash of booze once again." Officer Howard closed his notebook. "It's lucky they're both loudmouth drunks and couldn't keep quiet. They were behind the gift shop on Main, sitting next to the building, singing and laughing in a drunken stupor about what they'd done and how they were going to get the guy who locked them in."

"I guess stupid criminal tricks are real," Beau said gently.

"They really are." Officer Howard stood. "I'll let you know once we have the suspect in custody, but we have a good case, and once these men sober up, they'll be able to provide us with additional information, I'm sure." He tipped his head and placed his hat back on before walking out of the office. Dante heard Roberts in the hall and knew he'd see him out.

"This is such a mess," Beau said quietly. "My head hurts."

Dante locked his computer and stood to go to Beau. He seemed so tired. Dante lifted him off his feet, Beau resting his head on his chest, and Dante carried him up the stairs to lay Beau on his bed. He looked perfect there, and Dante hoped more than anything that he'd see Beau in his bed more and more often, hopefully on a permanent basis. But it was hard for him to let go of the guilt with what had happened to Allison and now all of this. How could one decision, made years ago, have led to all of this chaos and loss?

He turned to leave, but Beau caught his hand, holding it. "I know what you're thinking." Beau brought Dante's hand to his cheek. "I can hear that brain of yours churning."

"You do, huh?" Dante said gently, sitting on the edge of the bed.

"Yes. Somewhere in that brain of yours, you're making the humongous logical leap that Harper's actions are because of what you did with Allison."

Dante swore under his breath.

Beau chuckled. "I have really good hearing. Harper made his own decisions and took his own actions for his own reasons. He could have walked away at any time, but he didn't. Harper let his rage and anger consume him and cloud his judgment. None of that is on you." Beau lifted his head off the pillow. "I'm cold. Would you come over here and warm me up?"

157

Dante kicked off his shoes, climbed onto the bed, and slid up next to Beau.

THEY NAPPED a little, and Roberts knocked on the door at dinnertime. They had a light dinner in the bedroom and stayed curled up together.

Yates called late in the evening to say that he had a few possible organizations that were willing to donate space on a temporary basis for the Center.

"That was quick," Dante whispered as Beau rested next to him, eyes closed. Dante hoped he was asleep.

"I have some connections. I'm not sure if they will suit and we can look further, but I will send over the information, and you can have Beau look it over in the morning."

"Thank you." Dante lightly stroked Beau's hair. "The state police officer stopped by the house, and they have a good handle on what happened. Things seem to be happening fast."

"Good. I'll be in touch in the morning." Yates ended the call, and Dante set his phone on the nightstand, leaning against the headboard, watching a rerun of *The Big Bang Theory* on low volume.

"We should sleep," Beau told him quietly once Dante had turned out the lights.

"Just lie still for a while." Dante wasn't all that sleepy, and with Beau pressed against him, he was comfortable and warm. It was nice having someone in bed with him. Making love was one thing, but just being together, Beau putting himself in Dante's hands, was almost more intimate.

Dante watched the rest of the episode, and then they cleaned up and got ready for bed. He let Beau go first, and by the time Dante was done and rejoined Beau in the bedroom, Beau lay on his side, curled up under the covers, only his hair visible, snoring softly.

Dante padded around the bed, turned out the light, and then slid under the covers. Beau moved closer and then stilled, not waking at all. It was a little heady caring for someone this much, longing just to lie next to them in bed. It pleased him and terrified him at the same time. Dante wanted to accept that things between them were good. Everything he knew about relationships told him they were doing well. He trusted Beau, and Beau really seemed to trust him in return. It was almost too good to be true, which was about the time that everything went to hell.

CHAPTER 8

BEAU WOKE with a start at some point in the middle of the night. "Dante," he said, shaking his shoulders. "There's someone in the house."

"It's probably Roberts," Dante said groggily.

"No. Those aren't his footsteps on the stairs." He shook Dante's shoulder once more and reached over him to his phone.

"What are you doing?"

"Calling someone. Getting some help now," Beau said, becoming frantic. Whoever was outside was trying to move quietly, sneaking closer to their door. Beau grabbed the phone, pressed 911, and waited for an answer. He jumped out of bed and tried to get Dante to do the same.

Finally his call was answered. "What's your emergency?"

"Yes. There's someone in the house. I'm Beau Clarity, and I'm at the Bartholomews'." He grabbed Dante by the hand to get him out of bed, intending to lock them in the bathroom while they waited for the police, but the bedroom door burst open.

Dante ripped the duvet off the bed and tossed it at Beau as he turned to the intruder. "What the hell are you doing here?" Dante stood unabashedly naked to face Harper Bledsoe as Beau wrapped himself in the bedding, phone dropped and forgotten, and tried to race to the bathroom.

"Stop!"

Beau turned in time to see the gun pointed right at him. Even wrapped in the blankets, he was suddenly as cold as ice.

"You think you can replace my sister?" Harper's eyes were wild and his hand shook. Beau wasn't sure if it was fear or rage. Either was as dangerous as hell.

160

"I'm not, honestly." Beau tried to make himself appear smaller and willed his legs to stay under him.

"What is this rubbish?" Dante demanded. "Put that thing down before you hurt someone. What's gotten into you?" He stood rigid and tall, like a warrior of old.

"Rubbish! That's how you treated Allison. Like rubbish. She needed help, and you didn't do anything for her." Harper stepped forward, shifting the gun toward Dante. Beau didn't move an inch. He didn't want Harper to get more agitated.

"Dante. Please, sit down and let's talk." Beau was trying to be reasonable, hoping to defuse the situation and delay long enough for help to arrive. Thankfully, Dante took a step back, leaving his hands where they could be seen, and he carefully sat on the edge of the bed.

Footsteps sounded on the stairs, and Harper pushed the gun forward, toward Dante. "Tell them to stay away." He glared at Dante, who was clearly the source of his rage.

"Roberts, Beau and I are fine. Please go back downstairs." He kept his voice remarkably steady and strong. "Don't put yourself in harm's way." The steps hesitated, then retreated. "You have to know the police are on their way and the others in the house are going for help."

"I don't care." Harper blinked a few times, his pupils huge. Beau wanted to see him more closely, wondering what he'd taken. "I've wanted to get even with you since you got off for Allison's death. You killed her. Doesn't matter if you pushed her over the railing or not. You still killed her."

"What did I do?" Dante asked rather quietly. "Whatever it was, you have to know that I cared for Allison. She was my best friend for years. You know that." The pleading in Dante's voice was so unlike him. Beau wanted to comfort him but didn't dare. He tried to put more distance between him and Harper, but he was nearly at the wall. He probably could have made it to the bathroom, but he sure as hell wasn't going to leave Dante alone.

161

"She needed help, but you didn't get her any." Harper turned to Beau. "Neither did you—when she came to your Center, you didn't help." He waved the gun, and Beau caught Dante's gaze. He had no idea what Harper was referring to. "That Center. You all claim to help people, but you didn't help Allison. You're all the same—completely useless." The menace in his eyes, which had diminished slightly, returned full force.

Beau hoped to hell help arrived soon, because from the darkness in his eyes and the set of his jaw, Harper seemed to have determined that he'd had enough. Time was running out for the two of them. He turned to Dante, taking in the way he sat—tall and naked, but strong and almost majestic in the face of his end. Dante tilted his head just slightly, enough that Beau could see his eyes and knew Dante saw him. Their connection warmed him. Dammit, he didn't want to die. He wanted to spend years with Dante, grow old with him, and maybe they could have had children. So many possibilities flashed through his mind, but that's all they would be.

"I love you," Beau mouthed, and Dante blinked, his lips curling slightly at the edges where he could see them. What else did a person say at a time like this?

Suddenly the door opened. "Put the gun down!" A police officer stood partially in the doorway behind Harper in what looked like a state police uniform. "Right now!" The snap and power in his voice were awe-inspiring, and Beau jumped slightly. As a second officer joined him, this one wearing the blue of the local police, the state police officer stepped forward. "Harper, put the gun down."

"He killed her! He needs to pay!"

"We'll talk about it once you put the gun down."

The gun wavered, and slowly Harper lowered the pistol. The state police officer took it from him, and Harper was immediately taken into custody. As soon as he was out of the room, Dante sank down on the bedding like the fight had gone out of him.

Beau raced over to sit next to him, sharing the duvet to cover Dante up. "It's all right." Beau looked at the officer still in the doorway. "Can we get dressed?"

"Of course." The officer backed away, and within a few minutes, Roberts hurried into the room.

"We're all right."

"I called the police." Roberts fussed, keeping his gaze away to provide them privacy.

"Good. Thank you." Dante leaned close, dragging Beau into a hug. "This is just another consequence of my bad decisions."

Beau huffed slowly and returned Dante's hug. Then he looked at Roberts. "Please make some coffee. Dante and I need to get dressed. Let the officers know that we'll be down in a few minutes and that Dante and I want to speak with Harper before they take him away." If possible, it was time that the last of what had happened to Allison reached the light of day. Beau had an idea what had been going on, but it was only a theory. Maybe Harper was in the mood for some explanations and closure just as much as Dante was.

"I'll tell them," Roberts said and left the room.

Dante stood, the bedding falling away, and he got dressed, lifting his legs as though they were made of lead. "I don't want to talk to him."

"You aren't going to." Beau got the bag he used when he came to Dante's from the corner and dressed as quickly as he could.

"What does that mean?"

"That I am going to talk to him. I have some questions that I'd like to try to get some answers to, and you're the object of his hatred, though I suspect he has just as much guilt as you do. I suspect it was easier for him to turn the guilt into anger at you than to deal with it himself." Beau pulled on his shirt and then took Dante's hand. "I want you to wait outside the room. Other than knowing I'm your boyfriend, he doesn't have any other connection to me." Beau sat and waited for Dante, who seemed to fumble with the buttons of his shirt. Beau stood again and gently brushed Dante's hands to the side to take care of the buttons for him. "You were amazing when he burst in here. No fear and a tower of strength." He finished with the buttons and wiped imaginary lint off Dante's shoulders.

"I was scared half to death, and I knew I had to keep his attention on me. That way if anything happened, you'd have a better chance of surviving." He pulled Beau into a tight hug. "All I kept thinking the entire time was that I was going to lose you. I just found you not too long ago…."

"All I wanted was to give help some time to get here."

Dante nodded. "Why didn't he just shoot us and get it over with? He was out of his mind on something."

"Probably. His eyes were huge. But I think while his rage took over with whatever he was using, deep down he's not a killer, and that's what held him back. He was obviously angry, but you kept him talking, and mentioning his sister was genius. It reminded him of someone he cared for." Beau held Dante in return.

Dante touched his cheek. "I love you, Beau. I know this is probably a weird time to say it, but I do. I love you with everything I have, and if I'd had to, I would have given myself for you."

"I know that." Beau touched his lips to Dante's. "I love you too." He pulled away. "We need to get downstairs, because they aren't going to wait very long." Beau wanted answers and he wasn't sure how to get them, but he had to try. He would have held Dante like this forever if he could. They'd both had a scare, and Beau figured he'd fall apart once they were alone again, but right now he had something to do.

"Let's go downstairs so you can play Perry Mason."

Beau sighed and turned away to leave the room. They descended the stairs together, and Beau went into the living room, where the officers were waiting. Harper Bledsoe sat on the sofa, his hands zip-tied.

"Officer Howard," Beau said, recognizing him as the officer from upstairs. In the heat of the moment, he hadn't recognized him. Now that he could breathe, he easily did.

"This is very unusual, and we have advised him of his rights. So he may not talk to you at all." Officer Howard turned to Harper and then back to Beau.

"I don't want to ask him about tonight." Beau slowly stepped into the room and lowered himself into a chair across the way. He kept a good distance but wasn't going to be intimidated. "Upstairs, you said that we were all the same. That people at the Center didn't help your sister."

"You're all the same. You don't care." Harper pursed his lips.

"I've only been here six months and I never knew Allison, but everyone tells me how wonderful she was. So I have to wonder, what did she need help with?" Beau leaned forward.

Harper shook his head.

"I would have helped her if she had come to me." His gaze on Harper, Beau's eyes softened and then hardened once more, biting his lower lip. "I promise you, I have never turned anyone away. What sort of help did your sister need?"

Harper didn't say anything, and Beau began to feel that he was on a fool's errand. Whatever had happened and was the source of this anger, frustration, and guilt would stay locked away forever. Between Dante and Harper, those secrets were going to drive him to distraction.

"I only wanted to help." Beau stood and went to leave the room.

"Allison had surgery about four years before she died. She'd always had back problems. But they got worse, so she had surgery."

Beau slowly turned around at Harper's words. "Was it a success?"

"Yes. They corrected the vertebrae that were misaligned and pinching the nerve. But she was in a lot of pain."

Beau nodded but didn't move any closer. He didn't want to do anything to stop Harper from talking.

"They gave her pain medication, and after months, she was still in pain and taking the pills."

Beau nodded gently. "Did she become dependent?"

"Yes." Harper hung his head. "I tried to help her but didn't know what to do. She swore me to secrecy. I tried, I really did. I remember staying up with her on more than one occasion so she could try not to take the pills. I did try to help."

"I'm sure you did. But that kind of addiction takes a lot of help and is very hard to beat. I want you to know that." Beau swallowed hard, knowing Dante was listening even if he wasn't in the room.

"She didn't want anyone to know. Our parents wouldn't have been understanding. I know our mother would have taken the addiction as a personality failure of some sort. So we kept it to ourselves."

Beau understood. Addicts often were desperate to keep their addiction a secret from everyone in their lives. "Allison also had depression and—"

"Yes. She drank as well. I know that. I kept hoping she didn't take the pain pills with alcohol." The lines on Harper's face grew more pronounced. "I sent her to the Community Center because you keep things confidential. That's what I saw on your website. She went a few times and then said they weren't helping her." Tears ran down his face. The aggression and adrenaline from earlier were gone, having drained away, and now Harper was the picture of regret and loss.

"Was that before she married Dante?"

"No. It was after. She didn't want him to know either, but how could he not? They were married. They lived together. How could he not know that his wife was addicted to painkillers?"

"Did your parents ever find out?" Beau asked, and Harper shook his head. "Allison was obviously very good at keeping her secret." Beau almost stepped forward. He wanted to help. It was in his makeup to try to help people like Harper. "Dante knew Allison suffered from depression and he got her help. She was seeing a doctor for it." He wasn't going to go into anything more. "Thank you, Harper." Beau turned to Officer Howard. "I know what he did and that you need to follow the law, but please make sure he gets the help he needs. There have been too many lives ripped apart by what happened, and that needs to stop here."

"I'll do my best," Officer Howard promised.

"Thank you," Beau said quietly, watching as they got Harper to his feet and escorted him out of the room.

"We are going to need to talk to the two of you."

Beau nodded and left the room to join Dante, then led his shocked, wide-eyed lover away from the activity. Dante and Harper didn't need to see each other again.

"How did you know?" Dante asked. "You obviously led him to that admission."

They stepped into Dante's office, and Beau closed the door. "I had my suspicions, but I didn't know for sure." He swallowed hard and wanted to go to Dante, but he could feel him closing himself off. Dante sat in one of the chairs, looking at the floor.

"I didn't know. I thought she just suffered from depression, and I tried to get her help." He raised his gaze as Beau sat in the chair next to him, taking his hand. "But what I want to know is how you seemed to have it figured out and I never saw it. You didn't even know her."

Beau sighed. "When I first met you, I saw something familiar in you. Because I work with the families of substance abuse, I saw a lot of what I see in them in you. It's part of what told me that there was more to you than just your reputation. I could see the real man under the façade and pain." He felt his cheeks heat but pushed onward. "Anyway, after you told me about Allison, I went into her room."

A knock on the door interrupted him, and Beau groaned. He had been hoping to get all of this out into the open.

"Yes?"

Roberts poked his head inside. "The police are waiting for you."

Beau nodded and stood. "I promise I'll tell you everything as soon as we're done."

They left the room, Beau holding Dante's hand, and joined the police in the living room. With Harper gone, they answered all

ANDREW GREY

of the officers' questions as best as they could. There were some they could only speculate on, but they gave the police as much as they knew.

By the time they were done and the police had left the house, they were exhausted. Beau had trouble keeping his eyes open and sat on the sofa, holding Dante's arm, leaning on his shoulder.

"I almost lost you," Dante said in an ominous whisper. "I never want to go through that again."

"Me neither. No more lunatics through the front door." Beau blinked and closed his eyes once again. Part of him was afraid to sleep for fear of being attacked again, though the rest of him was too exhausted to stay awake.

"How did you know about Allison? I know it's late, but…."

Beau forced his eyes open and slowly got to his feet, figuring he could show him. "Come with me." He led Dante up the stairs, then past Dante's bedroom to the one next door. He opened the door and they stepped into the dusty, disused room that had been Allison's. Beau went to the bathroom and pulled open the medicine cabinet. He handed Dante one of the bottles inside. "OxyContin. Look at the pharmacy and the doctor." Beau left the bathroom and went to the bedside table, where he pulled open the drawer. He took out another bottle and brought it to Dante. "There's more, from a different pharmacy and doctor. They were filled three days apart." Beau waited for the realization to kick in for Dante.

"My God. How did I not know?" Dante held the bottles.

Beau understood. "Addicts are often very good at keeping their secrets, and she was probably convinced that she needed the medication. I'm willing to bet that there were other doctors and pharmacies. These are the only ones I found." Beau took the pill bottles from Dante.

"Allison was an addict?" Dante asked in what Beau thought might have been a sort of daze.

"Yes." Beau set the bottles aside and took Dante's hands. "I need you to understand that there were a lot of things going on with

168

her and Allison took her own life. I know you've felt guilty for a long time, but you have nothing to be guilty about. Allison had depression, and my guess is that she self-medicated with alcohol and pain pills. It's surprisingly common." He tugged Dante closer, engulfing him in the tightest hug he could.

"What does this all mean?" Dante asked.

Beau released him and guided Dante out of Allison's room, then closed the door. "First thing, it means that you have Roberts open that room and clean it out. Second, you stop feeling guilty about everything that happened. You didn't kill Allison, and regardless of what you thought all those years, you weren't responsible for her death. She was and no one else."

He got Dante into his bedroom and tugged off his clothes. It was the middle of the night and finally the house was quiet once again. Beau climbed into bed next to Dante, tugging him close and doing his best to try to soothe him. God, he hoped they could sleep, but he wasn't counting on it. He hadn't expected things with Dante to be quite this exciting. Hopefully the danger was over and the two of them could settle down a little.

BEAU WOKE the following morning to quiet, thank God. No phones waking him and no one bursting into their room brandishing a gun. Dante was awake, sitting up in the bed, covers pooled around his narrow waist. "What's going on?" Beau rubbed his eyes. "How long have you been awake?"

"Hours." Dante lay back against the headboard. "It's hard for me to believe that I blamed myself for everything for all this time and…."

Beau rolled over. "Did it ever occur to you that you kept secrets and took a lot of this on because you didn't want to hurt Allison's family? You did your best to preserve her memory for the people who loved her. That says a lot about the kind of man you are." He shifted closer. "But it's time you rejoined the rest of the world and stopped beating yourself up over something you didn't do. You weren't the cause of Allison's death. You tried to help her. If she had told you everything, you might have been able to get her the help she needed." Beau gently reached for Dante's cheek. He loved the scratchiness of his beard in the morning.

"Of course I would have." Dante leaned forward, pulling his knees up close. "She was my best friend, and I didn't know she was an addict. I had no idea." He leaned his head forward and grew quiet. Beau waited, and after a minute, Dante loosened up. Tears streaked his cheeks, and Dante pulled Beau to him, finally letting go of the years of pent-up emotion. Beau would never tell anyone that Dante cried on his shoulder. That was between the two of them, the ultimate show of trust. Beau held Dante's head, allowing him to let it out.

"I love you," Beau whispered, and Dante raised his face, his eyes puffy, his lips searching for Beau's.

"I love you too, and I don't want to be alone anymore." Dante's words came out hoarse. "This place is huge, and I… I want you here with me. I know it might seem like it's too soon, but…. You already spend your time here, and when you don't, I look forward to when you do…."

Beau held Dante as tightly as he could, pressing him back on the bedding, excitement coursing through him. "Of course." He missed Dante just as much when they were apart. "But just so we're clear, I don't want my own room." He smiled and ran his hands over the drying tracks on Dante's cheeks.

Dante smiled, a warmer and more genuine smile than Beau had ever seen from him before. "The Beast is dead," Dante whispered softly, almost to himself, and it touched Beau's heart to hear it. He'd known all along that Dante wasn't a beast and that the one person, more than anyone else, who needed to realize it was Dante himself.

"Well." Beau met Dante's gaze. "Maybe the Beast could stick around, but confine himself to the bedroom?" He wagged his eyebrows, and Dante laughed, unselfconsciously, before rolling Beau on the blankets and pressing him into the mattress.

"I think I can do that," Dante growled, and Beau let go, putting himself in the hands of the once Beast of St. Giles and knowing there was no one else he'd rather be with.

And he wouldn't change a thing.

EPILOGUE

The following January

"I DIDN'T really need a new tuxedo," Beau said as he struggled to fix his bow tie.

Dante stepped up behind him, and Beau's pants tightened just from his proximity. "Yes, you did. The one you had was at the end of its life." Dante reached around and efficiently tied the tie. "There you are. You'll be a wonderfully perfect host for tonight." Dante leaned closer to kiss his cheek.

"I wish I didn't have to."

"I know. But think about how perfect the new center is going to be." Dante turned him so he could look at him. "You've done an incredible job getting the new center designed and the city to use the insurance money to build it."

Beau scoffed lightly. "You put pressure on the mayor and didn't let him back out." Sometimes the Beast came out when needed.

"I still don't like that slimy bastard, but he did give the Center a long-term commitment on the space, so I'm letting the good people of St. Giles decide about him in the next election." Dante turned to the bed to pick up both black coats and hand Beau his. "Now we're raising money so the Center can be outfitted the way you want."

The ruins of the old Community Center had been torn down, and Beau had worked with the town to approve plans for the new structure. The shell of the building had been erected just in time for winter, and now interior work was well underway.

"I'm still hoping to bring in a psychiatrist so we can offer full medical facilities." Beau shrugged on his coat.

"Don't you worry. If you find someone, we'll work out an arrangement with the Foundation." Dante had already told him that so many times, but Beau wanted the Center to be self-sufficient. "And I know what you're thinking."

"You do, huh?" Beau grinned. "Fine. I'll accept your help as long as it's temporary." He melded his body to Dante's. "I never could say no to you, and you know it."

"Darn right." Dante grinned, his smile radiant. "Now, let's go downstairs and make sure everything is ready for company."

The tickets to the benefit had sold out in record time once Beau had announced it was being held at Bartholomew Manor. Beau hated the name and thought it belonged in the Batman movies. Still, everyone had wanted tickets. Dante had taken some convincing, but Beau had sold it on the fact that Dante needed to be seen, and opening his home, their home, for the benefit would help dispel more of the rumors.

"I really think we'd have been better off to have held this at a larger location."

"After this benefit, everyone will be talking about what a good host you are and how welcoming you were to everyone. They will not be talking about the Beast." Beau had made it his mission to dispel those rumors. They were firmly entrenched, but he and Dante were doing their best to give the people of St. Giles something else to talk about. Like the fact that they loved to walk through town, holding hands. Beau had figured if they were talking about how much they cared for each other, few people would have time for stories of the Beast. And it seemed to be working.

"All right. Let's go. Though I doubt there's anything to do. Between Harriet and Roberts, they'll have everything marshalled and set to go, I'm sure." Dante checked himself in the mirror, and Beau did the same. "You do look amazing." Dante stood behind him and leaned in close. "Though I can't wait to get you out of these clothes and into those sheets over there. That's where you always look best."

"Dante," Beau whispered, blushing hard, but pressed closer to Dante anyway. Sometimes he still found it hard to believe how Dante saw him, but Dante showed him all the time. Hell, he even sent him flowers he wasn't allergic to, and most days Beau worked from Dante's office because of the limited space in the Center's temporary location. But a flower delivery truck would show up anyway, just because Dante wanted him to feel special.

"Let's get downstairs now or we aren't going to leave this room." Dante hugged him closer, and Beau chuckled, knowing Dante was right. He stepped away and opened the bedroom door. Beau took Dante's hand, and they descended the stairs.

In preparation for the benefit, Beau had had the woodwork in the hall cleaned and the marble floors polished. They reached the main floor and went into the living room. Everything had been cleaned, polished, and buffed to within an inch of its life. Paintings had been cleaned and rehung, the chandeliers lowered and polished. The large dining room sparkled and glittered, set with canapes and small bite-sized morsels that Harriet had outdone herself with. The solarium was being readied as well, with a burst of greenery, indoor floral color of every variety, and fairy lights, and was serving as the bar for the evening.

The biggest change was in the ballroom, and as Beau stepped inside, he couldn't stifle his gasp. The chandeliers had been uncovered, as had the furniture. The Cabernet curtains, which had been taken down, cleaned, and rehung, were pulled back to show off the yard with fairy lights hanging in the trees. A platform had been set up at one end of the room, where the small orchestra would be performing.

"It's like the house has come back to life."

Dante squeezed his hand. "It has. You brought it back, just like you did for me."

"Is everything satisfactory?" Roberts asked, and Beau turned to him with a grin.

"This is stunning." He couldn't help trailing his gaze to the ceiling, with its mural and intricate plaster moldings. "Thank you for doing all this."

"It was my pleasure." Roberts hurried over to where the musicians were setting up, and Beau took Dante's hand once again to lead him toward the living room to sit until the guests arrived.

TWO HOURS later, the house was filled with guests talking and laughing, music flowing in from the ballroom to every other space, wrapping itself around Beau as he drank the last of his sparkling wine.

"Don't be nervous," Dante told him.

"I'm fine." Beau squeezed Dante's hand and stepped onto the small raised stage as the music faded, and he was handed a microphone by the leader. "Thank you all so much for coming."

The room burst into applause as Beau smiled, looking out at the sea of happy faces.

"As you know, we're in the process of rebuilding the Community Center, but I want to take a moment to thank the St. Giles Community Church for donating the use of their amazing facilities for us until we can move into our finished building."

There was applause again, and Beau waited for it to die down.

"Thank you. Tonight I have the privilege of unveiling the final interior plans for our new center." He looked at Dante and smiled, watching him as Roberts brought up the covered easel. "Ladies and gentlemen, it's my delight to give you the first look at the Allison Bartholomew Community Mental Health Center." Beau pulled back the covering so everyone could see the drawing of the front elevation for the new building. Applause filled the room, and Beau grinned, meeting Dante's dancing eyes. "Please, everyone, have a wonderful evening, and thank you for your support. It means so much to Dante and myself, as well as the entire community." He stepped off the dais and right into Dante's arms. Beau turned, and the orchestra started playing. "I need to check on—"

"Roberts has everything under control." Dante took Beau's hands, staring deeply into his eyes. "You've filled my life with happiness and love, and I don't know what would have happened if I hadn't met you."

Beau blinked away the threatening tears of joy. "You make me happy too, and damn it all, I love you with everything I have."

The music died away, and Beau realized he and Dante were in the middle of the dance floor, the room growing quiet.

Dante met his gaze and then slowly lowered himself onto one knee. "Beau," Dante began as Beau's mouth went completely dry, "every Beast has to have his Beauty, and I'd like to ask you to be mine for the rest of our lives." Dante reached into his pocket and pulled out a jewelry box. Soft gasps rippled through the room, but Beau barely heard them. All his attention was on Dante and the way his eyes sparkled and his lips curled into a smile warm enough to melt the polar ice caps. "Will you marry me and be my husband, partner, lover, and best friend?"

Beau opened his mouth, but nothing came out at first. Then he nodded deliberately. "Yes."

Dante slid a platinum and diamond ring onto Beau's finger and stood to tug him into a kiss that threatened to deepen by the millisecond. Thankfully Dante pulled away, and Beau blinked a few times. "God, I love you." Dante signaled, and the music started up. "Waltz with me."

Beau smiled, and he and Dante took their first steps in the dance and in the rest of their lives together.

ANDREW GREY grew up in western Michigan with a father who loved to tell stories and a mother who loved to read them. Since then he has lived all over the country and traveled throughout the world. He has a master's degree from the University of Wisconsin-Milwaukee and now works full-time on his writing. Andrew's hobbies include collecting antiques, gardening, and leaving his dirty dishes anywhere but in the sink (particularly when writing). He considers himself blessed with an accepting family, fantastic friends, and the world's most supportive and loving husband. Andrew currently lives in beautiful historic Carlisle, Pennsylvania.

Email: andrewgrey@comcast.net
Website: www.andrewgreybooks.com

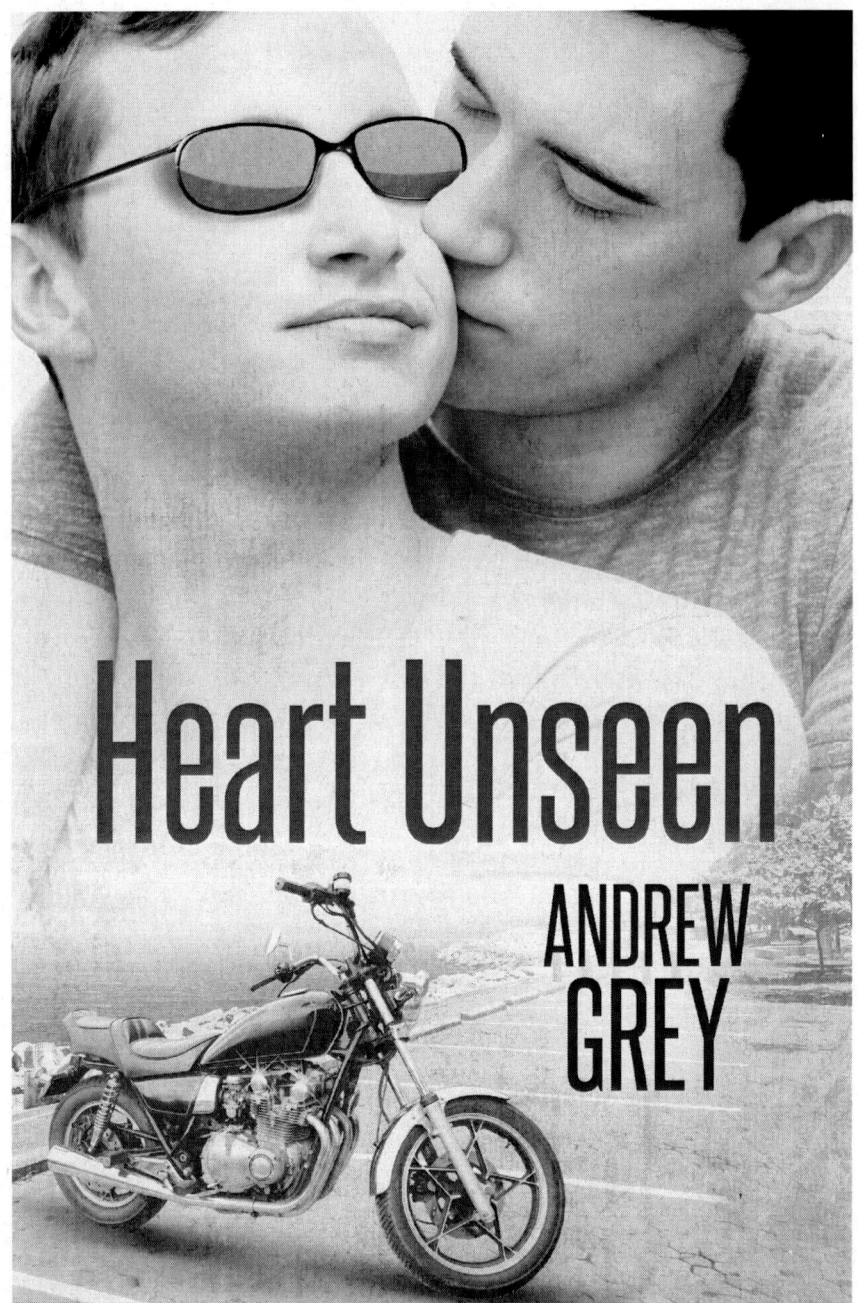

Heart Unseen

ANDREW GREY

As a stunningly attractive man and the owner of a successful chain of auto repair garages, Trevor is used to attention, adoration, and getting what he wants. What he wants tends to be passionate, no-strings-attached flings with men he meets in clubs. He doesn't expect anything different when he sets his sights on James. Imagine his surprise when the charm that normally brings men to their knees fails to impress. Trevor will need to drop the routine and connect with James on a meaningful level. He starts by offering to take James home instead of James riding home with his intoxicated friend.

For James, losing his sight at a young age meant limited opportunities for social interaction. Spending most of his time working at a school for the blind has left him unfamiliar with Trevor's world, but James has fought hard for his independence, and he knows what he wants. Right now, that means stepping outside his comfort zone and into Trevor's heart.

Trevor is also open to exploring real love and commitment for a change, but before he can be the man James needs him to be, he'll have to deal with the pain of his past.

www.dreamspinnerpress.com

DREAMSPUN
DESIRES

POPPY'S SECRET

Andrew Grey

A second chance born of love.

A second chance born of love.

Pat Corrigan and Edgerton "Edge" Winters were ready to start a family—or so Pat thought. At the last minute, Edge got cold feet and fled. Pat didn't bother telling him the conception had already gone through and little Emma was on her way. He didn't want a relationship based on obligation. He'd rather raise his daughter on his own.

Nine years later, Emma and her Poppy are doing fine. Edge isn't. He realizes what he threw away by leaving, and he's back to turn his life around and reclaim his family. It'll take a lot to prove to Pat that he's a new man, and even if Edge succeeds, the secret Pat has hidden for years might shatter their dreams all over again.

CAN'T LIVE
WITHOUT YOU

ANDREW
GREY

Forever Yours: Book One

Justin Hawthorne worked hard to realize his silver-screen dreams, making his way from small-town Pennsylvania to Hollywood and success. But it hasn't come without sacrifice. When Justin's father kicked him out for being gay, George Miller's family offered to take him in, but circumstances prevented it. Now Justin is back in town and has come face to face with George, the man he left without so much as a good-bye… and the man he's never stopped loving.

Justin's disappearance hit George hard, but he's made a life for himself as a home nurse and finds fulfillment in helping others. When he sees Justin again, George realizes the hole in his heart never mended, and he isn't the only one in need of healing. Justin needs time out of the public eye to find himself again, and George and his mother cannot turn him away. As they stay together in George's home, old feelings are rekindled. Is a second chance possible when everything George cares about is in Pennsylvania and Justin must return to his career in California? First they'll have to deal with the reason for Justin's abrupt departure all those years ago.

www.dreamspinnerpress.com

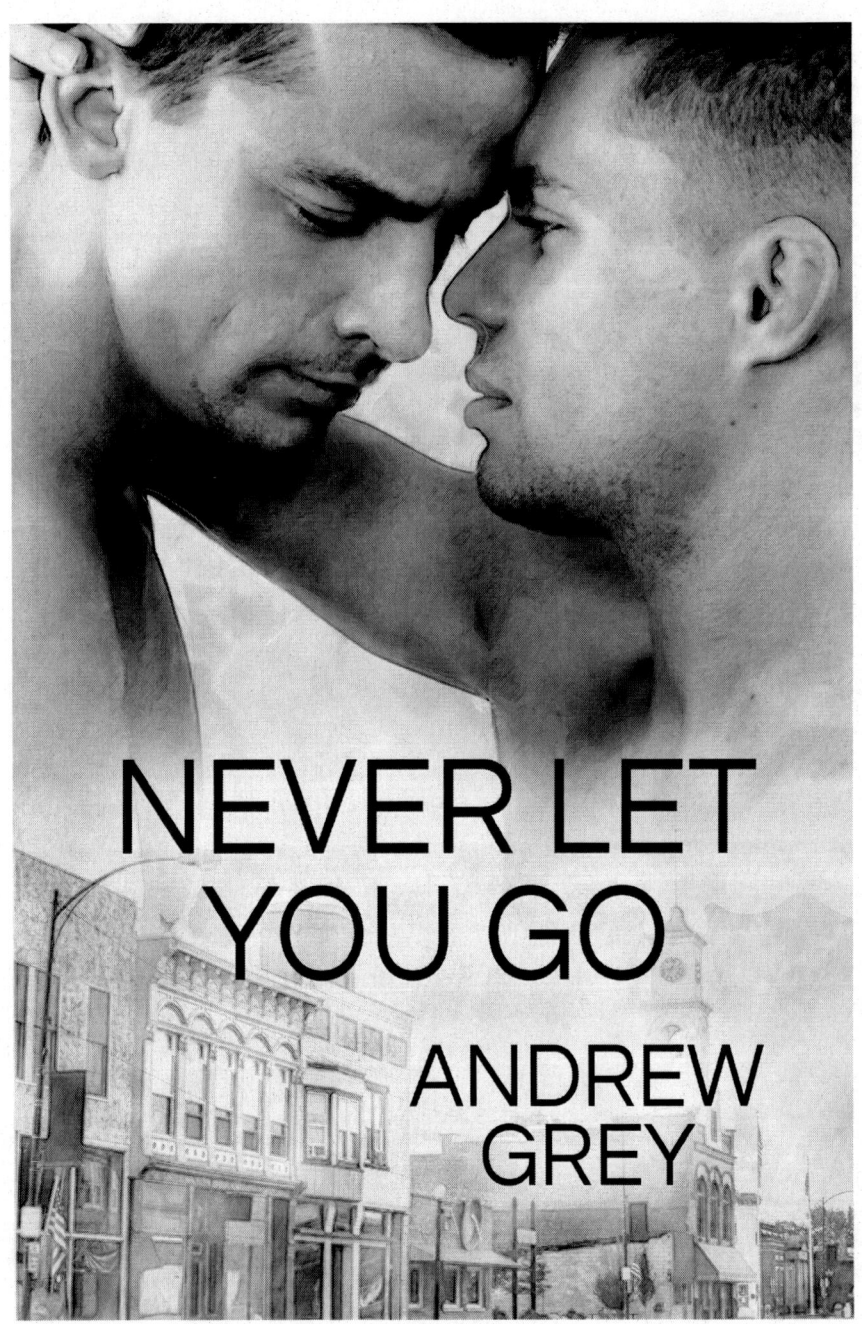

NEVER LET
YOU GO

ANDREW
GREY

Sequel to *Can't Live Without You*
Forever Yours: Book Two

Friends since they met in school, Ashton and Brighton soon become much more. Ash and his aunt are Brighton's haven away from his mess of a family, and when Ash enlists in the Army, Brighton learns to endure his long absences and eagerly awaits his return from missions.

Until one day Ash doesn't come back, and Brighton thinks his greatest fear has come true.

Months pass and Brighton grieves for Ash, not knowing that a terrible misunderstanding sent Ash running, unable to cope when he thought Brighton had betrayed him. Even after an emotional reunion, their relationship isn't the same—Brighton is now responsible for his young niece, and he's having a hard time rediscovering the trust he once had in Ash. Ash must still tend to his mental health, but before he can, he'll have to deal with a past secret that puts all their lives at risk. With so many forces determined to tear them apart, can Brighton and Ash hold on to each other and never let go?

www.dreamspinnerpress.com

SETTING the HOOK
ANDREW GREY

Love's Charter: Book One

It could be the catch of a lifetime.

William Westmoreland escapes his unfulfilling Rhode Island existence by traveling to Florida twice a year and chartering Mike Jansen's fishing boat to take him out on the Gulf. The crystal-blue water and tropical scenery isn't the only view William enjoys, but he's never made his move. A vacation romance just isn't on his horizon.

Mike started his Apalachicola charter fishing service as a way to care for his daughter and mother, putting their safety and security ahead of the needs of his own heart. Denying his attraction becomes harder with each of William's visits.

William and Mike's latest fishing excursion starts with a beautiful day, but a hurricane's erratic course changes everything, stranding William. As the wind and rain rage outside, the passion the two men have been trying to resist for years crashes over them. In the storm's wake, it leaves both men yearning to prolong what they have found. But real life pulls William back to his obligations. Can they find a way to reduce the distance between them and discover a place where their souls can meet? The journey will require rough sailing, but the bright future at the end might be worth the choppy seas.

www.dreamspinnerpress.com

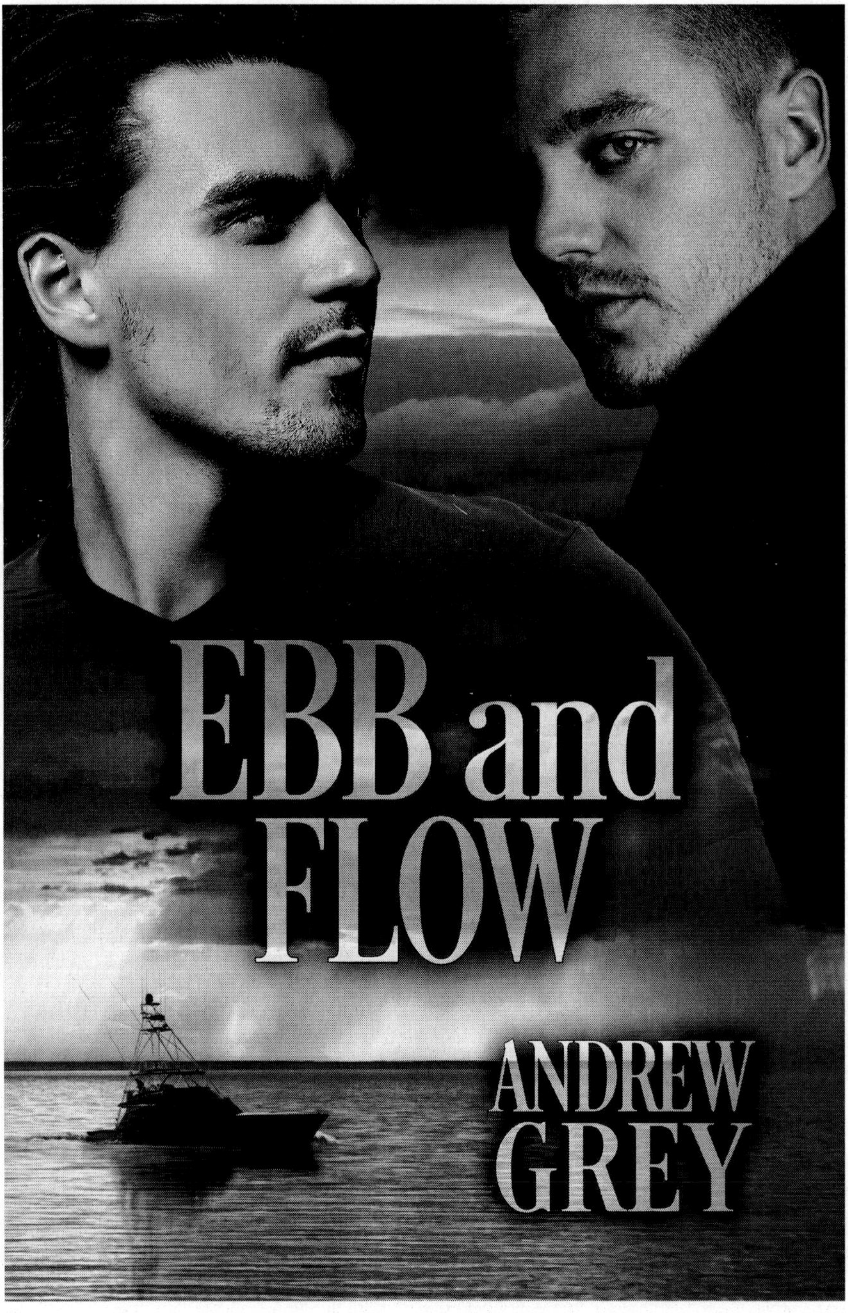
EBB and
FLOW
ANDREW
GREY

Sequel to *Setting the Hook*
Love's Charter: Book Two

To achieve happiness, they'll have to find the courage to be their own men.

As first mate on a charter fishing boat, Billy Ray meets a lot of people, but not one of them has made him as uncomfortable as Skippy—because he's drawn to Skippy as surely as the moon pulls the tides, and he's almost as powerless to resist. Billy Ray has spent his life denying who he is to avoid the wrath of his religious father, and he can't allow anyone to see through his carefully built façade.

Skippy is only in town on business and will have to return to Boston once he's through. After all, his father has certain expectations, and him staying in Florida is not one of them. But he doesn't count on Billy Ray capturing his attention and touching his heart.

Billy Ray doesn't realize just how much he and Skippy have in common, though. They're both living to please their fathers instead of following their own dreams—a fact that becomes painfully obvious when they get to know each other and realize how much joy they've denied themselves. While they can't change the past, they can begin a future together and make up for lost time—as long as they're willing to face the consequences of charting their own course.

www.dreamspinnerpress.com

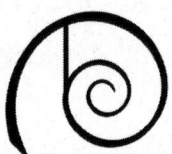

Manufactured by Amazon.ca
Acheson, AB

13481886R00111